Sergeant Goldsby and the 10th Cavalry

Fred Staff

Editorial design: Qolla Studio

ISBN-10: 1500347426
ISBN-13: 978-1500347420

About the cover

Artist and writer, Frederic Remington often rode and wrote about the 10th Cavalry. The media of the day treated black men as brutes or buffoons, but Remington's images were natural and genuine. He had a great admiration for the men of the 10th Cavalry. "The physique of the black soldiers must be admired – great chests, broad-shouldered, upstanding fellows..."

In a short story in Collier's in 1901, "How the Worm Turned," Frederic Remington responded to an early confrontation between troopers from Fort Concho and white criminals in San Angelo. His narrator reports how white Texans shot at black soldiers "on sight." After a 10th Cavalry officer was shot, he and his men rode in to settle matters. They entered the culprit's saloon, ordered a drink, then spun and opened fire.

"When the great epic of the West is written," wrote Remington, "this is one of the wild notes that must sound it."

This photograph shows an illustration from the Frederic Remington article in Colliers magazine, "How the Worm Turned," c. 1901.

DEDICATED

TO The

BUFFALO SOLDIER CHAPTERS ACROSS AMERICA

This historical novel is dedicated to the proud men and women volunteers who work tirelessly to keep the honorable name of the Buffalo Soldiers alive. Their efforts continue daily from Maine to Florida and from Texas to Washington. Their goal is to keep the great accomplishments and sacrifices of these brave and courageous volunteers in their well deserved spotlight. The service of the Buffalo Soldiers to America will not be forgotten, due to the hundreds of enthusiastic chapter members.

Their charitable, educational, civic and social efforts have done much to enhance the lives of thousands. They should be honored with the same zeal as the thousands, from the past, that they represent.

Chapter 1

The Beginning

The sun blistered the men and women out in the field, showing no mercy for those forced to toil for Master Winthrop. The only thing the hands had to be thankful for was that the end of the day was at hand, and the cool of evening would bring some long awaited relief.

George wiped his face with his tattered old red bandanna, and then removed his hat so he could pat the sweat from his short-cropped head of hair. Just like he did every day, he trudged up out of the deeply plowed rows of black soil and over toward the work shed. He put his hoe in its proper place and then headed to the living quarters with the rest of the slaves.

Boss Tucker roughly shoved his way through the throng of workers, knocking them aside as he bulled his way through the group, treating them like the worthless chattel that he thought they were. He chomped on the last moist remnants of a hand-rolled cigar in one corner of his mouth, and barked out of the other, "George, Mr. Winthrop wants you to come up to the house, and he said for you to be quick about it."

George looked up toward the house and saw Master Winthrop on the front porch, all decked out in his standard white suit and matching straw hat. He was a big man, and standing there with a drink in one hand and his mahogany walking stick in the other, he looked like the regal master of all that he observed; which he was.

George winced a little when he saw the mahogany stick. In his younger days, when he was still a little to headstrong for his own good, he'd known the pain of that mahogany stick across his back on more than one occasion, until he'd come to accept his station in life.

Master Winthrop plopped down in his large rocking chair. It was his throne, and where he enjoyed relaxing and surveying the workers in his fields. This was right where he could be found anytime the weather allowed.

Winthrop turned toward the door and shouted, "Damn it, Bella, get me another drink!"

George continued up the walkway, respectfully holding his hat in one hand, and still wiping sweat from his forehead with the other. He could see Bella rush through the door and serve the master a fresh drink from a silver serving tray.

Master Winthrop glanced up at Bella, setting his empty glass on the tray. She bowed toward him, and then when she turned to go back into the house, he grabbed a handful of her ample buttocks. She startled a bit and instinctively took a step away from him, but knew better than to show any other reaction of disapproval.

The master let out an ugly chuckle and looked directly out at George. His nasty grin was still on his face when George reached the porch.

"Right nice piece of ass there, huh?" Master Winthrop licked his lips, accentuating his depravity.

George didn't respond. He just looked down at the ground and waited for whatever the master would say next.

"George, set your ass down on them steps. I've got something to talk to you about."

George sat down on the second step. He knew better than to move up any further. From where he sat he still had to look up to the master, and he knew that was where he was expected to be.

"How would you like to have some extra rations and only have to work a half a day from now on?"

"Well, sir, that do sound good," George cautiously replied. He knew that rewards didn't come without a price, and he couldn't even imagine what the price for this generosity was going to be.

"I've been taking a close look at that baby girl of yours, and I think she's going to make a right pretty young woman. She came out nearly white, and I want a bunch of girls like that around her in the future, and I hate to say this, but you are one good lookin' man for a nigger. So I've decided to move you on over to the long house. I'm gonna move Bess, Carla, Cupid and Flower in there with you, and I want you to make me a bunch of babies." The master smiled a devious little smile as he laid his plan out to George.

"You know, George, my uncle just died and he left me his place to oversee for his widow. There's a fine bunch of young pickaninnies on his plantation, and I figured on movin' the best and prettiest ones on over here to put in the long house, so you'll have at least fifteen to do your business with in the near future."

"I don't want no messin' around with this. I want you to breed 'em all as soon as possible," Winthrop demanded.

George sat there for a moment, and then looked up at the master. He was a loss for words. He knew that this was a time when he'd better be damn careful about what he said.

"But what about Mable and my baby girl?" George asked.

The master smiled and said, "I think I'm goin' to move Mable in with the other girls in the main house, and I'll probably give that little one to Rose to rise. You know, you did a fine job makin' that little one, and I've decided that I could do just as good a job with Mable myself. There's a real market for light-skinned girls over in New Orleans these days."

George started to stand, but then he thought better of it. He was angry, and he knew whatever move he made might be his last. He realized that if he ever had the ability to convince a person to change his mind, this was the time to use it.

George looked down at the ground and wiped his head again. "Master Winthrop, I think the deal with 'em ladies sounds real good, but what I think might be even better is to move Mable in with 'em, and see if I can make another baby girl with her; maybe one even better than the last I made. I promise, I'll bust my hump tryin' to make all the babies I can for you." George knew he was taking a huge risk voicing his own opinion, but he thought it was a risk worth taking.

Winthrop rocked back and forth in his chair, considering George's proposition. He looked out across the fields and rubbed the palm of his hand against the afternoon whiskers on his chin. His silence kept George in an agonizing suspense.

"You know, George that might be an even better deal. I just got to thinkin', when Ashley Albright came up with that baby out of his wife's house girl, he got in more shit than a man should have to mess with. It seems that these Southern women don't like havin' little reminders 'round of what their men is doin' when they're out of the house. He got rid of that baby, and he's still payin' a price for havin' that little bit of fun."

"I think we just might do it like you said," the master agreed. "But I got some rules. First, you got to have 'em all bred in three months' time. If you don't, I'll get me some other buck in there to do the job and you'll be back in the fields all day, every day. Second, I'll leave Mable and that baby of yours in the long house. But understand this, George, and understand it good; I picked you because you're the best worker I got, and even more important, you're nearly as white as I am, and I want them babies to look like you because that's where the market is. But if you don't work out and get the job done, I'll just go buy me another light-skinned nigger that will," Master Winthrop threatened.

"I can still remember when my papa brought you here a few years ago. He had a real good eye for prospects back then and he said that you had the makin's of a great worker.

"I thought he was wrong 'cause you kept mopin' around all the time.

It took a little cane work and some time, but you finally proved he was right."

Those words brought back memories of that terrible time in George's life. He had been taken from his mother and his brother at the age of twelve, and the loneliness and loss had nearly been impossible for him to overcome. In fact, if it hadn't been for Aunt Bessie taking him in and teaching him how to survive, he couldn't possibly have overcome the desperation he felt.

George would never forget Aunt Bessie. It seemed like she had opened her arms and loved all those around her, no matter what their circumstances, and she always had just the right kind and loving words to fit any situation. Without a doubt, she was the main source of nursing and comfort for all of the slaves. She was a God send and the most respected person in the quarters. Everyone cherished Aunt Bessie and her undying love and attention.

The thing that burned in George's mind at the moment was what Master Winthrop had said about him being nearly as white as he was. He couldn't help but think that if he was nearly as white as his master, then why wasn't he nearly as free, as well.

Once again, an evil little smile crept across Winthrop's face. "The market is real good now since they stopped importin' niggers, and that new cotton gin has increased the demand for more labor. But the thing I figured out since I made that trip to New Orleans is that there is one hell of a market for light-skinned girls over there. You know, I can get right near fifteen-hundred dollars for just one unspoiled one. I aim to keep doin' the farmin', but I'm also going to turn this place into a real nigger factory. So, George, you better gets your ass in gear if you want to be part of the easy life.

Master Winthrop cupped his hand over the pearl knob of his walking stick and tapped it several times on the wooden porch, signaling to George that he was done with him, and he expected him to skedaddle on out to the quarters with the rest of the slaves until he needed him again.

George walked much slower than usual, dragging his worn old boots across the well worn lane leading over to the quarters. His head was spinning with the instructions he'd been given. The only consolation in this latest misery put on his life, was that he was going to be able to keep

Mable and his little Sarah with him. He couldn't even imagine what misery would have befallen Mable if the master had moved her within reach of his daily grasp. Most of the ladies up in the master's mansion were older women who did their job with skill. George was sure that Mable would have become nothing more than a plaything for the master, with him groping and grabbing her anytime he pleased when they were out of site of the lady of the house.

George had heard the stories from the mansion staff before, and he knew with time, Mable would have been forced to hike her dress and bend over a table or the edge of a bed and used as a comfort spot by the master.

Now his thoughts turned to Flower; one of the girls the master was planning to have him make a baby with. He knew her and her mother well, and he knew Flower couldn't be more than thirteen years old, and it just didn't seem right and proper for the master to use her like that. Besides, Mable was a close friend of Flower's mother, and he could only imagine the strain this new situation would put on their relationship.

The next thing that came to mind was that Bess was married; as married as a slave could be. She was married to Joe, and Joe was one of his best friends. What in the world would this new mess do to their friendship?

Cupid and Carla were young, pretty girls who George had known for a few years, but at least he didn't have any relationships with their families. He couldn't deny that the master had a good eye for the ladies, and he'd even been attracted to their beauty himself. But he and Mable had a strong relationship, and he hadn't had any desires to mess with anybody else because he valued what he and Mable had developed.

George's walk to the quarters seemed like it drug on endlessly. Just this morning all he had to worry about was getting to the fields and doing his work, and then getting back to Mable and baby Sarah at night. These new orders were causing all that to change and making his ways complicated and uneasy.

George entered the dark, drab interior of his small home, and was immediately greeted with a warm and loving smile from Mable. He

returned the smile as he walked toward her, and then pulled her against him in a strong, loving embrace. He held her against him longer than usual, and his warmth and care sent a message to Mable.

He finally released her just a little, and kissed her on the forehead.

As he'd done with his loving embrace, he held the kiss a little longer than usual, and then tilted her head up so that their mouths met. After a deep, passionate kiss, he released Mable and walked over and looked at his baby Sarah, sound asleep on the bed.

"George, what's wrong" Mable asked. "You sure do seem different tonight. You got somethin' you need to tell me?" Mable knew her man as well as any woman could know a man, and she felt something was deeply concerning him.

George looked down at the floor and then shuffled around the tiny room until he came to the edge of their bed. He sat down and patted the thin mattress, signaling for Mable to come over and sit beside him.

"I don't know how to tell you this, 'cept to come straight out and say it."

He looked at the dirt floor and paused before he could continue.

"Our lives is 'bout to change more than I ever thought possible. The master is gonna move us all up into the long house."

"Why's that, George? There ain't but the three of us. Why'd he go and do that?"

"Well," George explained, "There is gonna be a lot more than just the three of us."

Mable looked at him and asked, "George, did you go and do somethin' bad, and Boss Tucker is takin' away the house to punish us for it?"

"No, it's much different that than. Master Winthrop wants me to start breedin' women for the plantation."

Mable's heart sank with the weight of George's words, and her mind was filled with questions, but at the moment, all she could do was set in dazed silence.

After a moment, she looked up at George and asked, "What are you talkin' about? I don't understand what the hell you is sayin'."

George said, "It seems as if he has been lookin' at our Sarah, and he thinks she is just a perfect little girl, and he wants me to make more just like her. On his last trip to New Orleans he got some notions in his head that there is lots of money to be made by sellin' young girls to them rich bastards that live over there and the ones that come there for business."

The anger in George's voice was even more evident, and he said, "He wants me to breed a bunch of women for his profit, and he wants to make my children into whores!"

George slumped over and put his head into his hands, confused and ashamed and dejected.

Chapter 2

The Arrangement

The next few days, after Master Winthrop had laid out his latest plan to George, were filled with a flurry of activity. Boss Tucker had several men making new beds for the long house, and a handful of women stitched new mattresses. He had another group of workers moving in all the other new items that would be needed, and from the looks of things, Winthrop was quite serious about his new endeavor. By sunset on the third day, there were at least fifteen beds placed along the walls of the new house, and Mabel and Sarah were moved into their new home.

Being the first in the house, Mable got to choose which bed she wanted, and she chose the one nearest the back door so they would be next to the privy and the new kitchen area. It also provided as much air circulation as possible for relief from the oppressive Alabama summers.

She set about making the new surroundings as comfortable and as homey as possible. She knew that this new arrangement was going to be strange and uncomfortable for all involved, and just hoped that the more appealing she could make their new home, the better it would be for all of them.

Mabel's hard work made it obvious that she was determined to make the best of this unholy situation, just like she promised George she would do when he had given her the news of what new misery had befallen their lives.

She studied the huge room and gave thought to her next move. She couldn't figure out if she wanted the breeding bed near to her, or far away. She finally decided that the further away she located it, the better it would be.

At the front of the large room, she chose a place where there was a window on both the north and east side of the area. She made curtain rods from long cane poles and draped burlap bags over them that she'd stitched together, so they hung from near the ceiling to past the bottom of the bed mattress.

After she'd finished her handiwork, she studied the room and decided that she'd done her best to make the upcoming events as tolerable as she possibly could, no matter how unsettling she knew they'd actually be.

While she was admiring her work, George entered the room. He saw what she'd done; realized how difficult it must be for her to go through all of this, and a smile lit up his face as he lovingly looked at his woman.

"I know how hard this is for you, and I thank you for your work. In return, I promise you that I will try my damnedest to make this as easy on you as I can. Mable, I want you to know that no matter what happens in this house, I love you and only you, and I hate this situation we is in."

George walked over and wrapped his massive arms around Mable and gave her a long, deep, loving kiss."

"Now, I think the less we talk of this, the better."

Then he looked into her eyes and said, "Things has become bad for us, but it also has brung about changes that I never woulda thought possible. Boss Tucker has changed the way he acts toward me. Now he is decided that I'm an important part of this place, and that I've received some kind a blessin' from the master."

"When I ask him for something, he just seems to do anythin' he can to see that it gets done. I never woulda thought that I'd see a day like this, and it's takin' some effort to get used to."

"Boss Tucker has promised to keep us well fed and will probably even send a woman here to cook for the house. It is just amazin' how he's changed toward me. I guess he thinks I is now important and I aim to keep him a thinkin' that a way. You know, Mabel, maybe we can turn this into somehtin' we can survive with, rather than the hell we thought it to be."

The next day the new ladies were moved into the long house. As they entered, confusion was obvious on their faces. They had their arms full of everything that they owned, and they looked around their new surroundings, wondering what was going on.

Finally, Bess spoke up. "Mable, what the hell is goin' on here? Boss Tucker came in this mornin' after Joe went out to the fields and told me to get all my stuff gathered up. Is Joe goin' to be here this evenin'? We ain't done nothin' to cause us to be moved like this. What the hell is goin' on?" Her mind raced with questions.

Mable looked at all the ladies, and then walked over to Bess. She put her arms around her and tried to comfort her a little. As she did so, all the other ladies could see how nervous she really was.

After a long pause, Mable said, "Bess, we are faced with a real challenge here. I'm very uneasy dealin' with it, and I hardly know what to say."

Bess looked at her and said, "Well, I guess puttin' it off ain't gonna make it any easier. Just tell me what is happenin'."

"I know they probably told you that the ladies, in this house, were gonna be in charge of all the gardenin' for the plantation, and that's true," Mabel explained.

Bess interrupted, "Well, why did they have to move us for that? We can walk from our houses to the garden just as easy as we can from here."

Mable dropped her head, a little embarrassed for what she was about to have to explain, and said, "Well, that ain't all of it, and I jest don't know exactly how to say this. It seems that you ladies has been picked by Master Winthrop to...uh, to be the mothers of his next crazy work."

Mable looked up at the ladies again, and then stared up at the ceiling as she continued. She just couldn't bring herself to look them in the eyes when she told them the news. "It is the master's idea that George should make you all have babies."

There was dead silence in the room for several minutes as the women looked into each other's faces, trying to gauge how each one of them would react to the devastating news.

Bess dropped the armful of possessions she was holding. As they scattered across the floor she said, "What in the hell are you talkin' 'bout?

I's got a man and I's plenty happy jest the way we is."

Mable said, "I know...I know, and it is real troublin' to George and me too. But we has talked about it and decided that all we can do is make the best of it. I know that George has been workin' on how to handle this mess the best he can, and all you has to wait and hear what he has to say when he gets here. Now, I want you all to stop and think about it. We is the property of this crazy man and you know by rights he can do anything he wants to do wit us, and that includes killin' us if he sees fit. So before we all get in a fit about it, the first thing we gotta think about is how we gonna survive."

Cupid said, "This is real concernin' for me. Eli and I was jest about to ask the master to let us live together." She stumbled over to a bed and dropped her possessions and flopped down on top of her meager belongings and started to cry.

Mable rushed over to her and stroked her back, trying to comfort her, and said, "Baby, I know this is hard to take, but again, I want you to know that the first thing we gotta to do is survive. If it is any comfort to you, I promise that George is a kind and gentle man. I know that don't take the place of love, but we gotta do what we gotta do."

Now that the truth of it all had begun settling in, all of the other ladies had started to react as well. They'd all sat on the edge of the beds, their eyes hollow; staring into space like their souls had departed.

Carla spoke up, "We ain't animals. I don't care what the master says. We ain't animals. We got feelin's too."

Mable said, "I know we got feelin's and we know we'er better than this, but we gotta survive, and to do that we got to do what we is told. Don't you remember what happened to those two boys a while back...them two that said they weren't gonna work? If it hadn't been for Aunt Bessie and her carin' for 'em night and day, they woulda died from that strappin' they got. We sure don't want that for any of us, now do we?"

Carla looked at Mable and said, "I don't want to bring no child into this here hell. I am just thinkin' that I might as well die as to have a youngin' join me in this here hell."

Mable said, "I knows you all has got a lot to think about, but before we all get our mind closed to this, I suggest that we all set for a while and think on it for a bit. When George gets here I hope he can make you understand how upset he is with it all and how he hopes to deal with it. If you all will jest bid your time and try to think what best can come of it all, maybe George an make some of you feel a might better."

Chapter 3

The New Way of Life

George stepped into the house, carrying a large basket of vegetables under one arm, and a hind quarter of a pig under the other. He stood in the doorway for a few seconds, looking at the gathering of women. He slightly bowed a greeting to them, and then walked toward the back of the house. Passing by the women he could feel that they never took their eyes off of him. It was quite an unnerving feeling.

George laid the supplies down on the kitchen table, brushed off the front of his shirt, and then rubbed his calloused hands together.

George cleared his throat to speak, but it was so dry that the words just wouldn't come out. He turned to the bucket of water by the table and took a long sip from the gourd dipper.

He wiped his lips with the sleeve of his shirt, straightened up to his full height, and looked out over the group of ladies still staring at him.

He cleared his throat again, and softly said, "Well, ladies, I guess by now you've been told 'bout what you is here for. You all know that I love Mable with all of my heart, and what we are being' made to do don't set well with me."

"However, as Mable and I've talked, we must do whatever it takes for us to survive, and if that means doin' things we don't want to do, then we'll just have to get over it. I've somethin' to say to each of you, but they are things to be said in private. They will be words that I hope you take and understand that I have spent days thinkin' on. The first one I would like to talk with is

Bess. Bess, if you will come out back with me I'd be most obliged."

Bess hesitated, and then said, "Why can't you jest talk to all of us at once."

"Bess, each one of you have a different situation, and hopefully the plans I've made will help you understand what and why I' m goin' to do things the way I plan to do 'em. Now, if you'll come outside with me, I think you'll understand better."

Bess reluctantly walked out the back door with George following closely behind her.

When they got out of earshot of the others, George said, "Bess, you know that Joe and I are friends. You know that I wouldn't do anythin' to ruin' that if I could help it. So this is what I've decided to do."

"I'm not goin' to try and make babies with you. I'm goin' to let you pick a time of the night when you go to the privy. I will tell Joe the time, or some signal we can use; whatever works best, and he can meet you there. I don't care how you do it, but if you have to lean against the privy wall to make it work, then that is what you'll have to do. I'll let you meet like that for two months. If Joe hasn't got you bred by then, then I'll have to try, but you gotta get bred. That is the best plan I can come up with. The master has told me that I've got to have you all bred in three months' time, and if I don't, then he'll get someone else in here to do his biddin'. You gotta be careful doin' this. If you get caught, I got no idea what the punishment might be, but I am sure it will be bad, really bad."

"Now, do you understand why I wanted to talk to you alone?" George asked. "If they finds out I was a part of this they would skin me alive."

Bess stood in silence for a moment, looking up at George, and then said, "I understand, and I thank you. I'll be as careful as I can and I hope that me and Joe can make us a baby together. Now, I understand why Joe thinks so much of you. I promise that what we has talked about here will never be spoken of to nobody else."

"Bess, you do understand that from time to time you will have to share my bed? We can't even let the other ladies know that I'm not tryin' to put a baby in you," George explained.

Bess paused for a moment then turned to George. "Yes, I understand."
"Good, then just go on back in the house, and if any of the other ladies ask what we talked about, you can just tell 'em that we have agreed on a day for our get-together." George laid his strong hand on Bess's shoulder, trying to give her a little confidence in the midst of all turmoil that was happening in their lives.

Bess responded by reaching up and putting a small kiss on George's cheek.

"Tell Flower to come out now," George said.

Flower walked out the back door toward where George was waiting. She stared down at the ground, kicking the toe of her shoe in the dirt; apprehensive. In spite of her youth, it was evident that her young body was budding; her breasts full and hard against her light summer blouse.

She stood in front of George, folding and unfolding her arms, not quite sure what to do. She kept shifting her weight from one foot to the other;

unable to decide whether or not she should look up at George.

George reached out and placed his hand on her soft shoulder. He bent over so he could look directly into her eyes.

"Flower, you give me a great problem. How old are you?" "I's fourteen, I think."

"Do you know what they want me to do wit you?"

"I sure do," she said, and then she straightened up and looked more intently at George.

"Well, that makes me very uncomfortable," George said.

"Mr. George, don't fret yourself any. I knows what it is and Mr. Winthrop and both of his brothers has had their turns with me, and after it happened the first time, I kinda enjoyed it. So don't you worry none about me. I promise we can make a pretty baby."

George's mouth fell open. He rose up and was trying to think of something to say, but the words escaped him. All he could think about was the hours and hours he'd spent trying to figure out what he was going to do with this child; this child he thought had been untouched by such ugliness in her young life. Now, here she was, telling him she is more than ready and willing to be a part of this unnatural arrangement, and even more startling, that she might enjoy it.

"Damn it, girl, I want you to know that no matter what you say, it still bothers me a great bit."

Flower was swaying her hips from side to side and a smile lit up on her face. "I told you not to fret. In fact, I's looking forward to it." Even at fourteen years old, she knew the effect she was already having on men, and she knew how nervous she was making George. Even more, she was enjoying it.

George said, "Get on back in the house. Tell Carla and Cupid to both come on out here, and tell 'em to bring me a drink of water when they come."

George pulled up a short three-legged stool that was there for the women to use when they were sorting and preparing vegetables out back. He sat down and propped his elbows on the table and placed his head in his hands.

He thought about his conversation with Flower. He knew that young'un was going to be a problem, and that caused him great concern. His throat was so dry now that he didn't think he could even spit dust.

Both of the next girls come out of the house and walked over to George. Carla handed him a gourd full of water. George drank the cool water, never taking his eyes off the bottom of the gourd. When he finished it, he handed it back to Carla and simply said, "Thank you."

George got his wits back and looked up at the last two ladies and said, "Now, Ladies, you know what is expected of you and you know how it has to be done. Do you have any questions?"

"Cupid said, "Yes, we know how it's done. That don't mean we is happy about it, but we has decided that it has to be done and that we is gonna do what we has to do. The only thing we don't know is, when is it gonna be done?"

"Ladies, all of you will be workin' in the garden. Each day I will ask one of you to stay in with me. I promise, I will be as gentle as I can be, and hopefully we can get this job out of the way in as little a time as we can."

Chapter 4

Toby

Things in the house became much more comfortable as time passed. The ladies took their regular turns with George without any outward show of displeasure, and their initial fears were quickly laid to rest as they settled into the rhythm of their new way of life.

In line with Master Winthrop's new plan, George still had to continue with his other responsibilities in the afternoons, but because of the new status he'd gained with his duties in the long house, he was now promoted to a position as an overseer of the workers in the fields. He had to be certain that they were doing their work and taking care of the equipment that they were issued, and he was also in charge of the water boys and making sure that they delivered that most precious commodity in a timely manner.

Heat was a constant enemy of the workers in the fields, and as cruel and uncaring as he was; Boss Tucker knew the dangers of not keeping his workers hydrated. Many a worker had succumbed to the oppressive heat and passed out in the fields, and on a few occasions, some had even died.

Losing good slaves was never taken well by the master, so Boss Tucker was most lenient with the flow of water.

Aunt Bessie's son Toby was one of the many water boys. He was much too old for such a menial position, and he certainly had the body and strength to do much more productive manual labor, but mentally, he was still just a child.

All of the workers loved Toby and his simple-minded ways, and they always knew that when they were in need of a spiritual uplift, he was there to give it to them. He would happily run from worker to worker, delivering their thirst-quenching sip of water with a smile on his face that was just too infectious to ignore. Every worker knew that he didn't have any reason to smile, as he was enduring the same blistering Alabama sun that they were, but the fact that he could seem so happy in the face of such misery just made the suffering that they all faced just a little more tolerable.

George watched Toby go about his work and thought about how unselfishly kind Aunt Bessie had been to him, and what a true blessing she was to all of the workers. She had delivered almost every baby born on the plantation, and her vast knowledge of herbs and home remedies had soothed the pain and suffering of so many for so long.

George figured that having a son that wasn't right in the head had probably played a big role in making Aunt Bessie the incredible lady that she was. The fact that she could overcome what some would see as a burden of having a son like Toby, on top of the suffering she endured as being a slave, surely meant that she was an angel from heaven.

Thinking about angels brought the Reverend Thomas to mind. He came to the plantation every other Sunday in his shiny black carriage to preach salvation to the slaves. He waved his Bible in the air and in a loud and authoritative voice told them all how someday they'd be in Heaven with streets lined with gold, and how they'd have no more wants nor worries, but in order to earn that reward they had to obey their master and do all the things that he asked them to do.

To tell the truth, George knew that the only part of the service that the slaves really enjoyed was the singing, and that was another place where Toby set himself apart from the crowd.

There was no one in the group that could sing louder and more out of tune than Toby, and there wasn't a single person there that enjoyed the experience more than he did. In fact, not only did he sing the loudest, but Toby would break out in his hallelujah dance. Caught up in his enthusiasm, every slave there would start to clap and chant like they believed for just a moment that there really was a world waiting for them like Reverend Thomas preached about.

In spite of his situation in life, it was Toby's good heart that somehow brought hope into the lives of those on the plantation, even if was only for a few Sunday afternoons a month.

Aunt Bessie would grin from ear to ear and her eyes would light up with pride as she watched her boy motivate all the others. Everyone could tell that her heart swelled with pride when she watched her special son bring so much happiness to so many who suffered so much.

George shifted his thoughts back to the job at hand. The work was going well, but he noticed that there were more and more workers calling out for water. The shouts for water were common, but usually they were immediately met by one of the water boys jumping from row to row with a bucket of water in hand.

He looked across the field and didn't see any of the water boys tending to the parched workers; only men and women mopping their brows and fanning their hats and bonnets in the air in an attempt to get a little relief from the scorching sun.

At first George thought maybe the boys had gone down to the creek to get fresh water, but they'd never all gone at one time before. Now he was worried and broke out into a hurried trot down toward the creek.

Things had been going so well over the past few weeks that Boss Tucker spent most of the days sitting in the shade of the huge Live Oak tree over at the north end of the field. George noticed that he had an ample

supply of rum to comfort him, and he lazily lounged below the thick fingers of Spanish moss that draped down from the tree, and seldom ventured out into the blazing heat.

As George got closer to the creek he glanced back over his shoulder and saw that the yelling workers had got Boss Tucker's attention, and he was getting up to his feet and looking out across the fields to see what all the ruckus was about.

Boss Tucker struggled up into his saddle, straightened his hat on his head, and gave his horse a sharp bite of his quirt. He squinted hard when he moved out of the shade and the blazing sun hit his rum-glazed eyes. He was irritated at being disturbed, and the fuse to his short temper was lit as he rode toward George and the creek.

George knew this had the makings of a real bad situation, so he broke from a comfortable trot into an all-out sprint. Even before he reached the creek he could hear the boys laughing and horsing around, and his heart sank. Sure enough, when he got the clearing at the edge of the water he could see the boys splashing around and playfully slapping water at each other.

George shouted, "Damn it, boys! Get the hell out of that water and make it fast!" But he knew it was too late because Boss Tucker was closing in behind him, and no matter how quickly they got out of the creek, their water-soaked clothes would be a sure give a way to what they'd been up to.

As the boys scurried up the bank George said, "Damn, you boys are in a heap of trouble. Why in the hell did you have to go and do that?"

He'd just got the words out of his mouth when he heard Tucker's horse's hoofs thunder up behind him.

"What in the hell is goin' on here? What the shit are you no good bastards doin' in that creek?" Tucker was fuming. "You lazy black bastards are supposed to be carrying water; not laying around in it. I'll teach you a lesson you won't soon forget!"

George's mind raced, trying to come up with a way to defuse the situation, but he knew Tucker wasn't just mad; he was drunk. He'd seen him drunk too many times before and knew there was no reasoning with the man when he was in the grip of the spirits.

"God damn it! I'm gonna put a hurtin' on you little shits like you ain't never had before," Tucker yelled as he reached back and gripped the black snake whip he always kept handy at the side of is saddle. The whip was a constant reminder to the slaves of Tucker's expert ability to deliver quick and stinging punishment.

He shook the whip out to its full length and watched as the boys scattered and broke out into a run. Everyone seemed scared but Toby. Toby was the biggest and the fastest of the bunch, and as he raced by Tucker's horse he let out a little laugh as if he thought it was all some sort of a game.

Tucker reined his horse into position and gave chase, twirling the whip over his head to build momentum. When he was ready, he slung the whip out forward to its full length and let it wrap itself around Toby's body. He yanked it tight, pinning Toby's arms to his side and stopping him in his tracks.

"Ya got me, Boss," Toby said with an innocent little laugh, but before the words were out of his mouth, Boss Tucker raced past him at full gallop. The leather snake griped Toby's body even tighter and yanked him off his feet. His body slammed to the ground almost ten feet from where he'd been standing, and was immediately dragged; violently twisting and turning in the black Alabama soil.

All the workers turned their attention to the cloud of dust trailing Tucker's horse and the screams of pain that filled the air.

Tucker yanked back on the reins and pulled his horse to a stop, shouting, "Get up on your feet you son-of-a-bitch!"

Toby struggled to his feet, crying like the child that he really was. He bellowed, "I want my momma!" As soon as the words left his lips, Tucker tapped his heels to his horse and they moved forward, pulling the struggling and crying man-child behind him.

Toby crouched over and tried to resist the entanglement, but he more he struggled; the more he staggered and risked falling to the ground again.

"I'm gonna teach you and all the rest of 'em what happens when you slow down the work!" Tucker kept his horse at a brisk pace so that Toby could barely keep his feet under him. The more he saw Toby struggle, the bigger the menacing smile grew on Boss Tucker's face.

"Please, Boss...please...I want my momma!" Toby pleaded as he struggled behind the horse. Tears streaked down his pain-riddled face.

"You've pissed me off for the last time," Tucker replied. "I don't like your grinnin' nigger face and I never have!"

Now all the workers walked toward Boss Tucker and his captured victim. They were murmuring among themselves and greatly concerned for Toby's safety. They'd seen this brute in action before, and they knew what they were seeing now was probably just a taste of what was yet to come.

Boss Tucker jerked at the whip one last time, causing Toby to fall directly in front of the whipping post. He dismounted and marched over and kicked him hard in the stomach as he lay on the ground.

Toby grunted and rolled up into a ball; both hands grasping his stomach.

Tucker looked at the crowd of workers and ordered, "Joe, tie this bastard to the post."

Joe stood still. He dropped his head and didn't move an inch.

Finally, the man standing next to him said, "Joe, ya' better do what he says or more of us 'ill be next."

Joe stepped forward and gently helped Toby to his feet. It was obvious that it was tearing his heart out to be involved in this situation, but he helped Toby over and placed his hands on the part that formed the cross. He situated the restraints on Toby with as much care and kindness as he would tending to a little baby, and tears welled up in his eyes as he did what he was forced to do.

Keeping his eyes on the crowd of workers, Tucker hooked the black leather snake back to the side of his saddle; he did not use this killing device to administer punishment on the whipping post. He had whipped two slacking workers to death in the past with it and Winthrop had told him if he did it again he would take their cost out of his pay.

He then reached into his saddle bag and wrapped his hand around the thick metal handle of his specially made strap. His face was like a macabre canvas that showcased the devious pleasure he took in his actions.

He smiled as he let the six-foot leather strap roll out onto the ground. Without warning, he expertly flicked his wrist, sending the strap whistling through the air, tearing into the skin across Toby's exposed back, and barely missed Joe, who'd just finished the heart-rending task of tying the young man to the post.

Toby let out a scream that sent a chill through the hot Alabama afternoon. Then he cried, "Momma, help me!"

Then the second crack of the strap.

"Please, Momma, please." The words came as a whisper from Toby's lips now.

The strap cracked again and again and again, as it tore into Toby's back. Toby's knees buckled and he now was hanging with most of his body weight stretching his arms to their fullest.

The workers stood by and helplessly watched as punishment was ruthlessly delivered to this simple-minded boy, who had so often been their only source of hope an inspiration.

Suddenly, Aunt Bessie came bursting through the morose crowd. She stopped dead in her tracks when she saw Boss Tucker raining blow after devastating blow across he son's torn and bleeding back. She gasped in disbelief, and then rushed forward and grabbed the devil's arm before he could deliver another cutting strike of the strap.

Tucker yanked his arm free of Aunt Bessie's grip, and struck down with the blunt end of the metal strap handle against the side of her head. It was a vicious blow and her knees buckled and, as she dropped toward the ground he administered another blow to her head. She lit the ground without making a sound.

"Get this bitch away from me," Tucker barked.

He looked up to see who was going to heed his command, but instead of obedience, he saw hate in the eyes of two hundred men and women surrounding him.

Boss Tucker straightened his back and squared his shoulders to the crowd and said, "Well, I guess that is enough of a lesson for now. Get these two to the quarters and out of my sight."

He glanced down at Aunt Bessie, lying crumpled at his feet. Then he looked over to Toby's torn and bleeding body, hanging limp, still tied to the whipping post. "I said for someone to get these niggers over to the house, and don't you forget I expect a full work crew out in the fields, first thing in the morning."

Boss Tucker grabbed his horse's reins, and hurriedly pulled himself into the saddle. There was a little fear evident in his eyes as his foot searched for the stirrup. He had never seen the workers with so much hate in their eyes, and inside he knew that if they so decided that he was at a severe disadvantage. He kicked the animal's flanks and moved forward, pushing his way through the tightening crowd.

Everyone rushed to render aid to the two victims.

The first lady to reach Aunt Bessie reached down and touched her still body, and then slapped her hands to her face and screamed out, "Lord have mercy! Aunt Bessie is dead!"

She let out an almost inhuman wail of pain and anguish that gripped the crowd and sent chills up George's back.

"Aunt Bessie is dead," the crowd began to mutter, over and over, and then they all broke out into screams of grief, "Aunt Bessie is dead! Our Aunt Bessie is dead!"

The women cried almost uncontrollably as the others surrounded the body of the angle that'd lived among them, and the men stood silent, seething in their hate and anger at what had been done to their beloved Aunt Bessie."

George stood, transfixed by what was happening. Then he finally said,

"Damn it! Ya'll get Toby down and get him over to the long house. He's gonna need some serious tendin' to. Aunt Bessie is dead and you ladies is gonna have to get it done."

George had never felt like this before. He watched the men taking Toby's body down from the whipping post, and the thought about how sweet and innocent that young boy truly was. Then he looked over at the bereaved women as they tended to the lifeless body of Aunt Bessie. Now, he just felt cold; empty.

It was like he could feel every heartless lash that Toby suffered. And it was like his soul died right alongside Aunt Bessie when Boss Tucker pounded the life right out of her.

George didn't know for certain what his life was going to be like now, but he knew it was going to change. After the sun sat on this horrible day, George knew he'd be a different man. As many inhumane things that he had experienced nothing could come close to seeing the bastard Tucker snuffing out the life of the sweetest angle he had ever known. He swore that if there really was a God that he would surely give him an opportunity to take revenge for Tucker's actions.

Chapter 5

The Flight

Master Winthrop heard about the severe punishment Tucker had given Toby, and he also heard about him killing Aunt Bessie. He wasn't upset about Toby's strapping because he always gave Tucker the authority to deal with the workers however he felt necessary, as long as it kept the plantation in top production. However, he knew how the workers felt about Aunt Bessie, and he was very concerned that her death might stir up some long-held hostilities among the slaves. He'd heard several of them had used the word 'murder' when they talked about what happened to Aunt Bessie, but hell, white men didn't 'murder' niggers; they just punished them, and sometimes that had harsh results.

Winthrop thought he'd soothe the masses a little by having Reverend Thomas come and perform a special funeral service for Aunt Bessie. Unfortunately, it didn't do anything but rile the slaves up even more, because now they saw any and all white people associated with the master as just another one of their mortal enemies.

In the past, the slaves had come to accept their plight in life as best they could, but the violent and unnecessary death of the most beloved member of their group had created a hatred that was not going to be easily calmed.

Fearing that an uprising might be at hand, Winthrop brought in a group of about twenty hardened and well-armed men. He made sure these men watched over the workers day and night and extended them

the authority to do whatever necessary to quell any disorder against his dominion.

One of the smartest things Winthrop did was to get Boss Tucker the hell away from the plantation for a while. He knew his presence would be a constant irritant to the slaves, and he figured sending him off to his uncle's place for a while would make for a nice cooling off period. Either way, he'd already made his mind up that the niggers were not going to have any say in their treatment, no matter how just or unjust they might think it was. They were his property, and by God they were damn sure going to have to accept that fact.

Master Winthrop had the new boss call a general meeting of all the slaves, and made sure that they understood that in no uncertain terms, any sign of insubordination would be dealt with quickly and severely.

Things rocked along at the plantation about as well as Winthrop could expect. The work got done and the slaves behaved themselves about as much as they always had. It was obvious that their attitude wasn't the same; he could see the newfound hate in their eyes, but they kept in their place. So after about a month or so he brought Tucker back and placed him in charge again.

It was a long-held belief among all of the slave owners that any show of regret for any of their actions would be seen as a sign of weakness, and that was something they just couldn't afford to do.

As calm as things might have seemed on the surface, even after Boss Tucker was back in charge, the armed men were kept on site, just in case. And although he'd never felt a need to do it before, now Winthrop wore his own sidearm. When he walked around the slaves, he'd drape the edge of his white coat back over the pearl-handled butt of the pistol, making sure all of the workers saw it.

Now that Boss Tucker was back in charge, he returned to his heavy-handed ways, and made sure that all the slaves understand that any resistance under his watch would be immediately responded to with deadly force.

After the vicious strapping, Toby lingered on the verge of death for several days. Had it not been for the herbs and healing poultices that Aunt Bessie had taught Bess how to prepare and administer, he surely would have died. Even from her grave, it was his mama's love and wisdom that saved her son.

The strapping had done great damage to Toby, but the dragging had injured his intestines, and it had taken special care and a lot of luck for him to have survived. The fact he'd lost his mother made his recovery even that much harder. He refused to eat for quite some time and his continual cries of anguish made life difficult for everyone in the long house. It was a miserable and mournful time for all.

George had been successful with the first four women he'd been given to breed. They were all now were with child, and as an added bonus, Mabel was pregnant as well. It was clear that Master Winthrop was pleased and had plans for things to continue, because five more women were moved into the long house for George to service.

Even though things were going well with his duties in the long house, George was worried that in about seven months it was going to be obvious that he hadn't fathered the baby that Bess was carrying. Her secret nightly liaisons with Joe out by the privy had been successful, and since

Joe was as black as coal, George figured they'd just have to wait and see what Winthrop's reaction would be when the baby came out looking like his father.

Toby was finally well enough to return to his work in the fields. His personality had changed and he no longer smiled as he went about his duties; his loving spirit had been broken. He also didn't move as quickly as he used to because of a severe limp.

George kept a close watch on Toby, because he saw how he continually glared with unbridled hatred at Boss Tucker, and he wasn't sure how that might play out.

It was that time of the year that everyone began making preparations for the Winthrop Annual Gala. It was going to be an extravagant affair this year where only the cream of the crop of Alabama's social elite would be invited to the Winthrop plantation, and this year even the Governor was expected to be in attendance. Long days were spent decorating and painting every inch of the mansion. Food was harvested and brought in from all

of the fields and the ladies of the long house were assigned to prepare not only local vegetables, but also special and exotic fruits that had been brought in just for the big event. Some of George's ladies were required to spend as much as a half a day in the mansion to help the regular staff to assure that everything was ready for the big day.

The Winthrop Annual Gala wasn't just some afternoon picnic. Some of the families attending traveled great distances and stayed for an entire week. There would be dancing, drinking, card playing, and games for both the children and adults alike. Most of the men would spend their time smoking fine cigars and drinking rum and engaged in deep philosophical and political conversations.

In spite of the extra work required, George always looked forward to the gala. It was a time when he could mingle with the drivers of the teams that brought in all the other families. This was his only source of news from outside the confines of the plantation, and it was also a time when he could renew friendships from the past.

The one friend George was really looking forward to seeing this year was Joseph. He'd been a slave with him on the Goldsby plantation back before he was sold to master Winthrop. Joseph was several years older than George, but he always shared fond memories of George's mother and his brother, and George reveled in those precious recollections.

Joseph had done well for himself; at least as well as any slave could do. He'd worked hard and gotten himself out of the fields and into an inside position in the mansion of master McClain, one of the most influential of all the plantation owners. And with the help of master McClain's daughter, he'd also learned how to read, and that made Joseph one of the most valuable contacts that George knew.

The day of the McClain's arrival finally came, and George was thrilled when he saw that Joseph was the driver of that fine set of white horses pulling the most elegant carriage that he'd ever laid eyes on.

George went over and personally met their arrival, and while he never let on his familiarity with Joseph, he did smile to him as he assisted the McClain's down from the carriage.

George asked, "Can I help you with the bags and take your horses over to the stable?"

Joseph nonchalantly replied, "Yes, you can take that bag and we'll come back for the horses."

An air of non-familiarity was critical, because George and Joseph both knew that there were always eyes and ears about to monitor their every move. None of the masters wanted friendships to be developed between the slaves from different plantations, because they knew it might be the beginnings of some plot or uprising.

After the bags were deposited, the two men returned and unharnessed the horses and led them to the stable. It was only within those private confines that they finally greeted each other with broad smiles and the warm embrace of long-standing friendship.

"God, Joseph, I's so glad to see you. It's been nearly a year."

"No more glad than I am to see you, George. The last time we met was at this same gala, and too many things have changed."

"How's that?" George asked.

Joseph said, "I hear all kinds of things about a comin' war. The people of South Carolina are just itchin' to get out of the Union, and they is makin' plans to do just that. If I hear and read things right, it won't be long before the slave states will be in a tussle with the North and it could really be a big thing."

"You sure of what you been hearin'?"

Joseph turned and looked around the stable, making sure they weren't being overheard. "I heard Master McClain say that he and his friends has already started buyin' and storin' guns and ammunition. All of his relatives who is in the military schools has started comin' home, and some of 'em is even practicing on the weekends for a fightin'."

"How you think that is gonna affect us slaves?" George asked. His curiosity was peaked.

"Well, from what I hear from master McClain and his friends, is that we is the main reason for the war. It seems they think they have the right to own us, and a bunch of them from the North think they don't. This has been brewin' for a long time and it seems like it has festered as long as it's gonna. If what I hear is true, things is gonna break out like you can't even imagine."

"Well, I was expectin' news from you, but nothin' like this," George said with excitement in his voice.

Joseph said, "How this will affect us, I don't know. All we can do is waits and see. You know notin' may happen. Till that time we just need to visit. I want to know how you been, George."

"Well, I hate to say this, but Winthrop has made me a stud for his plantation. He has had me breedin' ladies as fast as I can get my trousers off. I's been pretty successful at it so far, and he just keeps bringin' me more girls to make babies wit."

"Damn, I don't know if I wouldn't trade places with you," Joseph said. "It sounds like probably the most enjoyable job there is around here." A smile crept across his face. "Sure beats the hell outa' hoein' and pickin'.

---How'd you get that job?"

"Seems like my light skin had a lot to do wit' it. He says he wants a bunch of light-skinned baby girls to turn into whores. I's really ashamed about that."

Joseph looked at George for some time and then said, "Well, I hate to be the one to tells you, but your dear momma was the daughter of a slave trader, and you are the son of Master Goldsby. That's why you're so light. I know it sounds real bad, but at least it seems to be servin' you well now."

That revelation set George back for a moment, and he was trying to figure out how to deal with this astounding revelation. He finally said,

"Well, I guess that answers some questions for me. I always had wondered why I was so light, and why I didn't have a papa around the house. My brother Crawford was as light as me; was he master Goldsby's too?"

"I don't know for sure, but I think he was the son of Goldsby's brother. I know they used to pass your mamma around a lot. You remember, she was one right good lookin' lady, and those horny old bastards just

couldn't keep their pants up when one of the good lookin' ones was around."
"Joseph, you remember Aunt Bessie?"

"Sure do what a fine lady. How is she."

"She's dead. That bastard Tucker kilt her. He hit her in the head when she tried to stop him from beatin' her boy Toby, and her killin' has sure changed the folks here 'bouts."

"Good Lord man I hate to hear that. She was such a fine lady and I remember she was like a mother to you."

"She sure was and to most of the folks here. Looked like for a while that things were gonna get ugly here, but I finally got the folks settled down, there ain't no way we could have done what we was a wantin' to. Winthrop brought in some bad men to see to it and all that would have happened was that a bunch of us would have probably joined her.

"You'll see them around here while the gala is goin' on. They still ain't totally relaxed."

Joseph returned to brushing his horses and said, "Well, time will tell what will happen and I hope it brings some relief to you and yours, but you better get for now and we'll meet again and talk more. Don't want them gettin' neverous about use bein' together."

The parties went on late into the night, and as a result of all the rum that was consumed, things often degenerated more toward the activities that might take place at a Roman orgy, than a gathering of Alabama's reserved and well mannered elite.

George and Joseph would set in the deep shadows of the huge Live Oak trees and watch groups of young men and women sneaking from one room to the next up in the mansion. It was almost comical to see the surprised looks on their faces when they'd cross paths with others who thought they were being so secretive.

Joseph finally chuckled and said, "George, I had a long trip and I'm tired. It's late and I'm goin' to bed. I will leave you here to watch, and tomorrow I want to know what the outcome of all this frolikin' around is." He patted George on the shoulder and slipped off into the night.

George watched about all he cared to watch, and was starting to return to the long house when he heard a rustling sound from the flower garden. He just assumed it was another couple who'd decided it would be more fun to indulge in their sexual deviances amongst the sweet smell of the honeysuckle vines.

Just as he was about to make the turn up toward the long house, a whispered voice called out, "George, George, come here."

He turned just in time to see Miss Daisy stumbling out of the flowers. She quickly glanced up toward the mansion, and then looked back at George.

"Miss Daisy, what are you doin' here? You should be in bed by now, and if Master Winthrop knew his daughter was out at this time of night he'd be havin' a fit. Let me help you back up to the house."

Miss Daisy staggered a bit, and then straightened herself upright and said, "That old bastard is long passed out from too much rum, so we don't need to be worrying about him."

"I's sure of that," George said, "but a proper lady shouldn't be out wanderin' around in the night, especially in your condition."

"It is my condition that made me want to find you," Miss Daisy said.

"Well, you can relax. I'll take you back up to the mansion, all safe and sound."

"That's not what I want. Some of my friends were telling me that the best poke they ever had was from one of their slaves, and I got to thinking that I got the best stud in Alabama right here in my own back yard." Miss

Daisy stumbled back a few steps and almost tumbled into the flowerbeds.

George reached out and grabbed her arm to steady her, and then just stood there in dumfounded silence. His head immediately turned from side to side, making sure nobody was overhearing this shocking conversation.

"What the hell you talkin' about, Miss Daisy?"

"I want you to poke me, George...right here and right now." George rushed toward her and put his hand over her mouth.

"Miss Daisy, hush up, please. Someone might hear what you saying'. I knows you had lots to drink and you is jus' not thinkin' right, so let me take you back up to the mansion."

Daisy brushed his hand away from her mouth and said, "I want you to take me, but not to the mansion. I want you to take me to the stable and put me in the hay and have your way with me."

"Damn it all, Miss Daisy, you know I can't do that. If they found it out they'd skin me alive and then they'd kill me, and I got no idea what'd happen to you."

Daisy staggered as she said, "I'm tellin' you, you are going to take me to the stable and give me what I want, or I'm going to tell them that you tried to rape me tonight."

"Miss Daisy, please. I knows you has had too much to drink and you is talkin' crazy. Let me take you on home now. Please, Miss Daisy."

"For the last time, take me to the stable and give me what I want or

I'm going to start screaming rape, right here and right now."

George knew he was in more trouble than he had ever been in, and he had never thought that such a thing like this might be happening to him. He knew he had to act fast, or sure enough Miss Daisy was going to get him killed.

He reached out and grabbed Miss Daisy's hand and said, "Come on then, and be quiet about it."

When they were finished, George stood up and brushed hay off of his bare chest with both hands, and said, "Miss Daisy, you can't be tellin' nobody about this or we'll both be in more trouble than hell knows what to do wit'.

Do you understand that?"

Daisy was still naked as the day she was born, sprawled out on the hay, illuminated by the moonlight that shone down through the stable windows. "Come on, George, let's do it again," she teased him.

"Miss Daisy, please, we gots to get you back up to the mansion before we both gets caught. Please!"

Daisy sat up and grabbed her clothes and started getting herself together. "All right then, but you listen up, George. Let's get one thing straight. I own you, just like my daddy does and I will use you any time and any way I want," she said as she struggled into her clothes. "If I want you to walk me down to the creek, or tell papa that you have to take me into town in the carriage, you're going to do it. The other girls do with their man slaves as they see fit, and I aim to do the same thing with you. So you just go on back to poking your nigger women, but remember this; I get what I want, and when I want it."

George reached down to take her arm so he could help her back up to the mansion. Daisy jerked away from him and said, "Let go of me, nigger. I'm done with you for now. I can see my own way home."

George was filled with more fear than he had ever believed possible.

He couldn't even comprehend what he'd gotten himself into now, and he knew there was no way that any of this mess was going to end up in anything but an absolute disaster for him.

The next few days, George felt like everyone who looked at him knew exactly what he'd done with Miss Daisy. Anytime Boss Tucker or one of his men looked at him, it was like they were looking right into the depths of his deepest, darkest secret.

As time passed, nothing unusual happened, and he started to feel a little more relaxed, but in the back of his mind, he always knew that at any moment his world could explode in disaster.

Late one afternoon, just as the sun was setting, marking the end of another long workday, George was standing near the end of the field rows and watching as the workers picked up their tools and headed towards the shed. All of a sudden, Toby limped by him with a hoe in one hand and an empty bucket in the other. George couldn't figure out why Toby was going for another bucket of water at the end of the day, but it wasn't unusual for Toby to do strange things, so he didn't give it much thought.

But then he saw Boss Tucker kick his horse into a trot and head right toward where he'd seen Toby disappear over the ridge through the Willow trees to the creek.

When Tucker trotted past George on his horse, George fell in right behind him, following him down to where Toby was. When they reached the clearing by the creek, George crept into the stand of Willow trees where he could watch what was going to take place. He knew Tucker still had a grudge against Toby for the discipline he'd received over him killing Aunt Bessie, and George knew things could get real bad, real fast.

Tucker dismounted and drew his pistol. He crouched down and skulked through the Willows low hanging branches, moving toward the creek bank as he stalked Toby.

Toby rose up once he'd filled the bucket in the creek, and turned to walk back toward the fields. Tucker stood up and leveled his pistol directly at him.

"I finally got you tryin' to run away, you ignorant nigger." I've been waitin' for this chance for a long time, and you finally ga ve it to me."

Toby looked at Tucker and said, "No sir, Boss, I's just gettin' some water to take up to the house. I ain't goin' no where but back to help the ladies fix supper. They ask me to bring this here water when I come."

"That's what you say. I say you is runnin' away, and to keep you from doin' that I'm gonna kill ya'. You been the cause of most of my troubles and the best way to fix a problem is to just get shed of it."

Even in the deep shade of the willows and the fading sunlight, Toby could see the evil grin that crossed Boss Tucker's face.

Just as Tucker started to cock back the hammer of his pistol, George stepped out from behind the willows and said, "Boss, I promise you, Toby ain't gonna cause you no more problems. You know he ain't right in the head, and if you'll let him go, I'll keep him up at the long house and have him help the women with their work. You won't never even have to lay eyes on him again."

Tucker glanced over at George, still keeping the pearl handled pistol leveled at Toby's chest. "It's too late for that. This idiot done got himself in the spot I've been waitin' for, and today is the day I'm getting' rid of his black ass once and for all. If you know what's good for ya', you'll get on back up to all them women of yours and make some more babies."

George dropped his hands to his sides and turned like he was leaving, but suddenly reached out and gripped the pistol by the cylinder to keep it from rotating. He pulled at the gun in an effort to get it away from the Boss, but all he got for his efforts was the Boss's arm around his neck from the back. Tucker's forearm was now deep up under his chin and he was able to reach over and grasp the forearm of his gun hand, allowing him to apply great force on George's neck.

George kept his hold on the pistol, still trying to save Toby's life, but before he knew it his world was going dark and he was losing consciousness. He didn't even remember dropping to the ground, or letting go of the pistol.

When George came out of his chocked state, he was staring up into the caring face of Toby. He tried to get up and catch his footing, but he was still too disoriented to steady himself.

Toby said, "Don't worry, George, it's all right. Just rest there a spell. I done good."

George propped himself up on one elbow and could see Boss Tucker laying over on the creek bank with the heavy blade of the hoe buried deep in the back of his head. Dead.

"My God, Toby, we is in a world of shit now." "But I done good, George, didn't I?' Toby asked.

"Well, you probably did, but that want fix this mess."

Toby sat down next to George and said, "I done good, George. I know I done good."

"Toby just let me think a bit...just let me think," George said, and patted his hand on Toby's back.

After a few minutes George said, "Well, we're lucky that the creek is up and runnin' strong. Help me get Boss Tucker into the water and hopefully it'll carry him on downstream a bit and give us a little time to figure out what we gonna' do."

They got Tucker's body wrestled into the water, and then raked as much of the bloody sand and gravel as they could down into the creek as well.

"Can you ride that horse?" George asked.

"Sure can. I can ride good. I always wanted to ride Boss Tucker's horse."

"Well, Toby, you got one chance. It's comin' on dark now and you've got to get on that horse and head south. Listen to me carefully. Don't run that horse to hard or you'll end up on foot. Ride him til' sun-up, and don't go near no towns. Don't stop at no houses and do your best not to get near none. Let the horse drink anytime you feel thirsty; he'll be thirsty too. During the day, you hide in the woods and don't you come out for nothin'.

You understand me?"

"Sure thing, George, I understand good. Don't ride him none too hard, let him drink when you'er thirsty, and don't go near no towns or houses. Oh yeah, and hide in the woods when it's daylight. Sure thing, I understand good."

"You'er gonna' get hungry, but unless you can steal something at night, or find something in the forest, you just stay hungry until you get somewhere safe."

"Okay, George, I won't eat none unless I can find it in the woods. I don't wanna be stealin' nothing."

"Toby, this ain't no game we're playin'. You'll be a dead man if anyone sees you, so you do what I say. I'm gonna give you Boss Tucker's pistol. All you gotta do is pull back the hammer and pull the trigger, but don't you shoot it les' you just got to."

"Okay, George," Toby said, and he reached down and picked up Boss Tucker's revolver from the creek bank.

"Now listen, you should get to Florida in a few days. There are Indians there called Seminoles that will take you in and help you. I've been told that lots of slaves live with 'em. You gotta get to 'em, Toby, you understand?"

"I can do it, George. I know I can. But I done good, right? I done good, George."

"Yeah, Toby, you done good. Now don't forget none of what I told you. Just keep ridin' south and don't talk to nobody til' you get to 'em Seminole Indians in Florida."

Toby got up into the saddle. He sat there proud as punch, and it was the first time George had seen him smile since the day Boss Tucker gave him the strapping, and the day his mama died.

"It be a good horse, and I can ride it all the way to Florida. I be seein' you someday, George."

Toby tapped his heels to the horse's flanks, and rode out to the south.

George knew Toby's chances of actually making it all the way to Florida weren't too damn good, but at least he'd given him some kind of chance at surviving. It sure was more than he had if he stayed on the plantation.

Now, George scratched his head and wondered what the hell was going to happen when everyone realized that Boss Tucker and Toby were both gone.

"Damn it to hell," George said. "Goddamn it all to hell."

Chapter 6

The New Challenge

The next morning George was back to his normal duties, watching the workers as they gathered their equipment and went about their usual tasks in the fields. Not a single one of them seemed to give any thought to the fact that Boss Tucker wasn't in his usual place.

The hired enforcers showed up, and as usual they lounged around under the shade of the Live Oak tree, waiting for Tucker to take his usual position with them. They laughed and joked and from time to time would cast an eye over toward the workers, but they too seemed unconcerned that Tucker hadn't appeared.

After a couple of hours one of the enforcers finally got up and walked over to the mansion. A few minutes later he wandered back to the group hanging around in the shade, with Winthrop tagging along beside him. They were talking and pointing and carrying on about something in a lively conversation.

George kept a wary eye on the master and his hired guns, wondering if they were discussing the whereabouts of Boss Tucker. He didn't have to wonder for long.

"George, get your ass over here, and hurry up about it," Winthrop hollered.

George trotted over toward the men, and as he got closer he removed his hat and said, "Yes, sir, master, what can I do for you?"

Winthrop motioned with his hand for him to get closer, like he didn't want the other slaves to hear what he was about to discuss. "Have you seen Boss Tucker today?"

"Na sir, I seen 'em last night ridin' out on that fine horse of his. I think he said somethin' about ridin' to Selma. I didn't think too much 'bout it 'cause just that afternoon he was tellin' me that I wasn't the only one getting' to play with a passel of women. He was braggin' and rubbin' it in 'bout havin' a couple a sisters over in Selma that just couldn't get enough of 'im."

Winthrop kicked the toe of his boot at the ground and said, "Well, I'll be damned. I never would have thought that Tucker would let a little evening delight get in the way of his work, but maybe he's in over his head with those women."

He turned and winked at his hired guns and they all broke out into a raucous laughter.

Winthrop turned to the man that seemed to be the leader of his occupying force and said, "Send a couple of men into Selma and see if you can round up ole' Tucker. He hasn't never neglected his responsibilities here before, but I guess I'll have to excuse him a little, but only if he decides to share his good fortune with us."

Again, the gruff group broke out into smiles and laughter.

Master,if you don't minds, I need to get up to the house," George asked. "I got all those women out workin' in the garden, 'cept for the one that needs breedin', and I figure she's good and ready right about now."

"Well, George, then get your ass on over there and give her a few pokes for me, too."

Once again, the men shook their heads in approval and let out a roar of laughter.

"Yes, sir," George said, and took off in a trot toward the long house like he was about to be hard at work for the master.

When George entered the house, Flower was laid out naked on the bed.

"Not today, Flower. Get your clothes on and go put your tit in that baby's mouth. I'm not in the mood today."

"But I'm ready...more than ready," she moaned. "You ain't poked me in nearly a week and I's be needin' it more than that."

"Flower, I'm tellin' you, not today. I got things on my mind and I ain't got time for none of your nonsense. Now get on outa here and tend to that baby. I'll do you good and hard tomorrow, okay?"

"You promise, George? Good and hard, 'cause you know that's what I like." George didn't see the need to reply. The last think he needed on his mind today was the nonsense of a young girl.

No one had heard from Tucker and his absence had not seemed to change the daily lives of the workers. Another thing that appeared to be going George's way was the fact that the new men had not been around long enough to have noticed Toby and the way he worked. Therefore, his absence had not brought about any questions.

George stepped out on the back porch of the long house. The sun was smothered with thick white clouds today, so it seemed like it might be a little cooler than usual. He watched the ladies putting the finishing touches on preparing the noon meal, and just tried to enjoy the moment.

He looked up toward the mansion and noticed an open carriage coming up the plantation road. It was being pulled by a team of fine white horses, and he immediately thought of Joseph. As the carriage neared, he was sure that it was Joseph driving the team, and he smiled. Maybe this was going to be a good day after all, he thought.

George was delighted to see Joseph again, and like always, he hoped he could catch up on news from outside the confines of the plantation.

He'd only been able to hear bits and pieces about the plans for war from the hired guns since the last time he and his friend had been together, and he was hoping that now Joseph was here, he could fill him in on everything that was really going on out in the world.

He ambled over toward the mansion to help tend to the arriving visitors. He thought that it was a little strange that McClain would be coming in the middle of the week for a visit, but regardless of why he was coming, he was just glad that Joseph was going to have time to share

When the carriage pulled up to the front of the mansion, George reached up and grabbed one of the horse's bits so he could guide the team over to the hitching post. That's when he noticed the lone horse tied to the back of the carriage. He stepped back to get a better look at the animal and his heart skipped a beat.

Damn, it was Boss Tucker's horse. He was sure of it. How in the hell did McClain get that critter? George's mind raced. Then his knees got weak and he couldn't even acknowledge the smile his friend Joseph was sending his way.

Now, George was even more concerned about why McClain was making this unannounced visit. He tied the team up so they could get water, and then walked back over to where Joseph was. As he wiped his hands on the front of his trousers, he noticed McClain stepping lively up the steps of the mansion.

George whispered, "Joseph, what the hell is going on with that horse?" He tipped his jaw up to indicate Boss Tucker's steed.

Joseph nonchalantly replied, "A bunch of horse traders came by the plantation the other day and they had that one there in their string. Master McClain recognized the brand and asked them where they got it, and they said somewhere down by Mobile. Master McClain thought it would be the friendly thing to do to bring it home to where it belongs.

"That's it?" George asked.

"Yep, simple as that. Just the friendly thing to do. Why you ask?"
"Boss Tucker is missin', and that there is his horse...that's why I'm a askin'," George said.

"I heard something about that," Joseph said. "But I thought he was chasin' some ladies over in Selma, then just disappeared. Least that's the story I heard."

"Yeah, that's what I heard too." George took a deep breath of relief. "Maybe he just got his horse stole and was too ashamed to come on back."

"You know, Master McClain thinks maybe he got bushwhacked and they took his horse," Joseph added.

George hesitated and thought about that for a moment. That might make the story even better for him. "Yeah, you suppose that's what he's gonna tell the master?"

"I'm plum sure he's gonna tell him what he thinks," Joseph said. "Why you so worried 'bout it. You talkin' like you lost your best friend or something, and I know you got no good feelin' for that that man." Joseph was starting to get curious about why George was so stirred up about seeing Boss Tucker's horse.

"Well, it's just been weighin' on my mind a bit, that's all. Let's just forget 'bout it and visit a spell," George said.

Joseph smiled. "Sounds good to me. You know, you ain't even said a proper hello to your old friend."

"Damn, I'm sorry. What a terrible way to treat a friend. You'll have to forgive me, Joseph. I just got some things on my mind and I hope they don't turn into somethin' bad."

"Well then, maybe what I gots to tell you will get your mind off your troubles. The South boys has done gone and started the war."

"What?" That tidbit of news caught George completely off guard."

"Yep, them boys went and fired on a fort on the river and it looks like there is really gonna' be some kinda war. The best part is, they is fightin' to set us slaves free."

"Are you for sure? Is you tellin' me the truth, Joseph?"

"From what I hear, them people from the South they be callin' Confederates, say they ain't talkin' that kinda treatment from them Yankees up north, and the fightin' is on."

George couldn't believe what he was hearing. "And you say it's 'bout settin' us free?"

"That's what I hear, and there sure has been a lot of people comin' and goin' at the plantation, and they is all actin' like they is stirred up and ready to get right into the middle of the fight."

George thought about that for a minute. "You know, the master has been goin' out a lot lately and comin' home real late. He's been havin' a real look a concern about him and drinkin' more than usual. I was wonderin' what's been eatin' on 'im, and I bet that's it."

Master McClain and Winthrop stepped out on the porch and sat in the big rockers, and one of the house girls came and served them two drinks off a silver tray. George and Joseph glanced up and noticed that they seemed to be deep in some serious conversation.

After about an hour, the two masters stood up and shook hands, and McClain came down the walkway toward his carriage. As he got close to the horses, he turned back to Winthrop and said, "Now remember what I told you. We're going to be counting on you for at least twenty."

Winthrop nodded his head and raised his glass to McClain and replied, "You can count on me, and I'm ready to give more if needed."

McClain climbed up on the carriage, and Winthrop hollered after him with one final thought. "By the way, I have eight new uniforms bein' tailored right now. I can't wait to get back into the action, and especially for such a good cause."

McClain leaned out of the carriage and said, "I didn't tell you, but go ahead and have a star placed on those new uniforms. The committee met and decided that with your experiences in the Mexican War, we'll be needing leaders like you." He waved and Joseph snapped the reigns and the carriage headed down the road.

Winthrop had a smile that could light up the night as he waved a parting goodbye to McClain. Then he lifted his glass toward the sky and immediately put it to his lips and drained it.

He placed the empty glass on the tray and said, "George, come on up here a minute," Winthrop hollered over the sound of the carriage wheels crunching down the gravel path.

George sat on the porch step in his usual position and Winthrop said, "George, this thing about Tucker is really starting to weigh on my mind. You told me you saw him going toward Selma, and yet his horse shows up over near Mobile. I know you probably haven't heard, but they found his body in the river down by Selma. He'd been in the river so long that the only way they recognized him was by those fancy boots he always wore. Them catfish had had their way with him. I'm thinking there might be more to the story than what you said. You sure you don't have anything else you need to tell me?"

"No, sir. I done told you all I know," George said with a deadpan face. "Maybe he got himself bushwhacked or somethin', and they just slung is body in the river and stole his horse."

"Yeah, maybe," Winthrop agreed. He always had a little poke with him and he sure liked to play cards." Winthrop scratched his chin and thought about that a little. "Yeah, maybe that's what happened."

"Something else, George. What about Toby. The reverend said he hasn't seen that boy at preachin' for several Sundays, and he's wondering what happened to him."

"You know, sir, after his mama got kilt', he didn't want to go to preachin' no more. He ain't never been right in the head, and after that beatin' Boss Tucker give him and his mama getting kilt', I think maybe he just wandered off or somethin'," George explained.

Master, I is sorry I didn't tell you before, but Toby has been a actin' so strange lately that I just figured he's show back up any day now. You know he don't know how to fix for his self, and I figured when he gets hungry enough, he'll probably wander on back home with his tail between his legs."

"Well, he wasn't much good for anything, anyway. I guess it don't really make no difference...we ain't lost much," Winthrop said. "Ok, George, take Tucker's horse on over to the stable and brush him down good and then get him in the corral with the rest of the horses. At least I can salvage something from this mess."

"Yes, sir! I'll take real good care of 'im."

George led the horse over to the stable. The further away he got from Winthrop and his questions, the calmer he felt. Those questions were starting to hit too close to home, and he feared that his past was about to catch up to him.

George also figured that the master's excitement about being promoted to a General might have kept him from digging to much deeper into lesser matters, and at least for the moment, that was a blessing for sure.

The situation with Toby never raised its ugly head again. Master Winthrop seemed satisfied with the notion that he'd just wandered off. George felt confident that Toby had never made it to Florida and the safety of the Seminole Indians, and just figured that he'd been killed somewhere over by Mobile. As much as he hated the thought of Toby's death, he was actually relieved to know that he hadn't been captured and forced to tell what had really happened with Boss Tucker.

Nowadays, George was somewhat of a celebrity around the plantation. When Master Winthrop had military men or dignitaries come to visit, he'd call George up to the house and parade him around and brag on him.

"Boys, take a look," Winthrop would gloat. "There's the truth standing right in front of you. If you breed strong men to good women, you'll get the kind of workers the south needs now and in the future." He'd tip his drink towards George like he was some kind of prize livestock.

George resented being paraded around like a blue ribbon bull, but because of his celebrity, he was privy to conversations that few slaves ever got to hear. Mostly he'd hear Winthrop complaining because he and his men were assigned to supply and transportation duties. He continually criticized the powers to be, and claimed that he was a fighting man, and that his skills were needed in the heart of the battle, and not tending to a general store on wagon wheels.

No matter how much Winthrop complained to his visiting superiors, they always said that his work was critical in making sure that necessary supplies were delivered to the right place when needed, and that his fine efforts were a big part of enabling the South to continue to march forward, despite their many defeats on the battlefield.

Winthrop continually expressed his dislike of no fighting and keep reminding the visitors that he and Lee were not only friends, but that they had roomed together in military school and that if anyone knew how to support him in battle it was him.

Winthrop accepted their praise, but he never believed it. In his mind, he knew he would better serve the cause by leading men into the perils of battle, and defeating the enemy head on.

It was at one of those very meetings when George was being paraded around, that his life took a drastic change. Winthrop was ordered to deliver a huge load of food and war materials up to Vicksburg, and he was told that Vicksburg was the key to holding the Mississippi, and that if fell, Jefferson Davis believed that the war would be lost for the South.

Now, Winthrop had something he could sink his teeth into, and he dove into the responsibility with a newfound vigor. He spent days on the road, mustering a string of supply wagons and filling with everything needed to hold the Mississippi.

It was early May and the weather was a mixture of oppressive heat and pounding rain. The master called for George, and said, "Looks like you have all the women either suckin' babies or their bellies are full. This is going to be a hard trip and the weathers not going to make things any easier. I'm going to need all the strong men I can get to get my duty done. I'm taking you and Joe with me, George, and I want you to pick twenty other strong men to take with us to keep the wagons in shape and help push us through to Vicksburg. Your work here on the plantation can wait a bit. For now, we gotta' win this war." Winthrop spoke like he believed he was the driving force behind the war now, instead of a just a supply clerk wrangling wagons full of war goods over miles of muddy roads.

"Yes, sir," George said, and he went about preparing for his new duties with mixed feelings. He truly hated leaving Mable and his two 'real babies' behind, and he'd also grown quiet fond of many of the other babies that now filled the long house.

On the other hand, he was thrilled to think about having the chance to get off the plantation and see the country. In his mind, it was almost like getting just a little taste of what freedom might really be like.

The trip to Vicksburg took fifteen days, and all in all, it went on without a hitch. There were a few river crossings that were a little difficult because of rising waters due to the seasonal rains, and most days were spent pushing and dragging overloaded wagons down mud-bogged roads, but it was nothing George and Joe and the twenty others couldn't handle.

When they arrived at their destination, they were greeted with sights like nothing they'd ever expected. The city was abuzz with workers; most of them slaves, constructing all sorts of fortifications and trenches to protect the city. It was a city getting ready for war, and everyone was doing everything possible to prepare to withstand the hell they knew was coming.

Once there, George and the rest of the plantations slaves were put to work with the others, preparing to hold off the fury of the coming Union army.

George noticed that Winthrop began acting strange after word came that Lee had been successful in the battle of Chancellorsville. He paced the floor and couldn't sleep and wandered around muttering about how he was missing the fight, and how he had to get to Lee and help him drive the Yankees out of his homeland.

Then suddenly, Winthrop announced, "I have over one hundred men that should be in the fight, and I am taking them to help our beloved General Lee! By God, he and he alone can save our great land and he needs all the help he can get!"

With that declaration, he ordered all of the wagon drivers and all the other men under his command to load up and push forward at a breakneck pace toward Virginia.

Most of the men had mixed feelings about the trip. Some were excited that they finally might actually get into the heat of the battle to protect their beloved Dixie, but at the same time, they were a little concerned that Winthrop was acting more and more like he was losing his mind.

Winthrop drove the men at an unmerciful pace, and barely allowed them rest or sustenance. He seemed not to need sleep or food for himself, and constantly threatened to have men shot for insubordination when they requested even a moment of time to rest or eat. He was obsessed, and it was taking a heavy toll on his men.

To everyone's surprise, the made it to Virginia. What was even more amazing to most was that they'd passed unscathed through territory that was heavily occupied by Union troops, and they hadn't even come close to encountering hostile fire.

The men mumbled among themselves that it just goes to show, with a little faith God takes care of those who can't take care of themselves. They were convinced that Winthrop had lost his mind.

It was now early July, and as Winthrop and his men arrived to their staging area, there was no doubt that the war was in full swing. The sounds of cannon and musket fire filled the air.

Suddenly, Winthrop seemed to change into an entirely different person. Not only did he allow it, but he encouraged the men to prepare a good meal, and then he demanded that they get a good night's sleep.

When their bellies were full for the first time since they'd left on this arduous trip, and they were preparing to bed down for the night, Winthrop stood before his men and declared, "Tomorrow, you sons of the South will show those Yankee bastards what real men are. You will fight for your homes and your families, and you will slaughter those who have tried to destroy our way of life. Some of you will surely die, but you will die with glory, and there is no death more revered than one sacrificed defending what a man believes in. Now, rest and prepare for a great day to come."

George and the other slaves bedded down for the night, but there was no way they could sleep with the continual thunder of cannon and rifle fire.

At the break of sunrise, Winthrop was marching about camp in a crisp new general's uniform, swinging his sword like he was chopping the heads off sunflowers in the fields. He shouted to his men, "Follow me!

We've got the bastards trapped on that ridge over there, and we will put an end to this war today!"

He led the men behind a long split-rail fence and they joined up with what looked like thousands of gray-clad soldiers. He stood and looked across an open field that was nearly a mile wide, and pointed his sword at the ridge on the other side.

"The bastards are there. They lay in fear of the South, and today we will put them out of their misery!"

While Winthrop was bellowing to his men, several real battlefield generals rode by on their horses, wondering who in the hell this crazed madman was, but they just kept on riding.

The ground continued to rumble under constant barrage of Confederate cannon fire, and the men could see great clouds of dirt and debris bursting from the ground all along the ridge where Winthrop had been pointing toward all morning.

To the surprise of the Confederate soldiers, the Yankees stayed silent, not returning fire. Word moved up and down the lines that the Yanks were out of ammunition, and it was going to be an easy victory. Spirits soared and there seemed to be an early sense of triumph in the air.

A little after noon the rebels crossed the split-rail fence and let out a blood curdling battle cry as they broke into an all-out run across the meadow toward the ridge.

George huddled behind the fence with the other slaves, and was absolutely amazed at what he saw.. He'd thought that there were several thousand men at the ready, but now that he could see them all running across the field, he realized that there were far more heading into the battle.

General Winthrop was running tall and proud, right along with the regular soldiers. He was swinging his sword and yelling out battle orders at the top of his lungs. Nobody seemed to be paying any attention to him, but he seemed to be having the time of his life.

When the onslaught of Confederate soldiers got about a quarter the way across the field, the ridge became alive with smoke and fire from the

Yankee cannons, and in just seconds, the meadow was covered with dead rebel soldiers.

General Winthrop was leading at the front of the horde of troops, and he was one of the first to hit the ground. He lay there face-down for a moment, and then rolled over onto his back. He lifted his sword high into the air, and then his arm fell limp to his chest.

George and the other slaves watched in disbelief as hundreds of those who charged the ridge under Winthrop's orders fell under a fury of heavy cannon fire, and then as countless others were cut to pieces by relentless volleys from the muskets.

George finally realized that now the heaviest action was far in front of where Winthrop had fallen, and he decided to go out and bring him back.

George and Joe ran across the battlefield in a crouched position, dodging stray musket balls that whizzed past them. When they reached Winthrop, they grabbed him by his arms and legs and drug him back to the safety of the fence line.

They placed him on the ground and looked at the blood that flowed from the two wounds that he had received. He was motionless for a moment and then looked up at his saviors. "Well, looks like you niggers done good and saved your old master," Winthrop said.

George looked down at Winthrop, and all his years of enslavement flashed before his eyes. He recalled all the many beatings at the hands of this cruel man; even those he'd gotten back when he was in mourning over the separation from his dear mother. He remembered all of the inhuman treatment that the master had approved and encouraged for Boss Tucker to deal out to keep his niggers in line. He thought about all the deaths of so many of the slaves and his friends that this man owned, and of course, he could never forget Aunt Bessie and the cruel treatment of the innocent Toby.

George looked around to be certain that the other men were too busy fighting or just trying to survive, and couldn't notice what he was doing with the master. He pulled the master's sidearm from his holster and said, "No, sir, we brought you here so we could make sure you was dead. But before you go, I want you to know that you are goin' a be a grandpa. That's right, you're sweet little Miss Daisy is goin' to have a little nigger baby, and I be the daddy. I'm afraid that if I let you live to see it, and that baby is a girl, you'd be tryin' to poke her just like you done to so many others, and I just can't be havin' that. I also want you to know that you is the worst man I ever known, and I'm riddin' the world of you right now."

Winthrop's eyes widened. He even made an effort to rise. As he struggled to get to his feet he yelled, "You nigger son-of-a-bitch, I'll kill you with my bare hands. There is no nigger going to live and talk to me like that. You lying bastard, my Daisy wouldn't have a damn thing to do with your black ass."

"Well sir, you may think that, but if you were home you could see her risin' belly, and I want you to know that I put it there, and she enjoyed it greatly."

George cocked the pistol and pushed it hard against the master's head and pulled the trigger. He didn't hesitate and he didn't give it a second's thought.

Joe was in shock. He couldn't believe what he just witnessed. "Goddamned, George! What'd you just do? What the hell we gonna' do now?

"Tell you what, I'm 'bout to fall in that ditch over there and run like hell toward those blue coats over on that hill. If you and the others got any sense about you at all, you'll fall in right behind me."

George stuck the master's pistol in his belt and sprinted toward the ditch. He could hear the others' feet pounding on the ground right behind him. Once they all got in the ditch, they kept their heads low and made their escape as fast as possible.

After they'd covered several hundred yards the ditch made a sharp right turn and as soon as George made the corner he was confronted by four gray-clad soldiers huddled down behind the embankment.

The confrontation was a shock to both the rebels and the slaves, and for a brief moment they just stood and stared at each other. George grabbed for the pistol in his belt before the rebels could react and ordered, "Don't move a inch or you is dead."

The men immediately threw up their hands, and one of them asked, "What the hell is you doin' with a pistol, nigger?"

George leveled the pistol at the rebel and said, "I be plannin' on getting' the hell outta here and joinin' 'em boys in blue, and I don't aim for nobody to be stoppin' me."

The rebels looked back and forth at each other for a moment, like they were validating a common goal. Then one finally said, "We done seen all the killin' we aim to, and we been tryin' to figure out how to surrender without lookin' like cowards and deserters. Would ya' take us with you."

George gave it a minute's thought and the said, "Put your hands up in the air and leave your rifles against the side of the ditch. Walk out in front of us and don't even think about lookin' back til we get to 'em Yankee boys over there."

As much as George hated the rebels and everything they stood for, he decided it might be a good move to show up at the Yankee camp with a batch of prisoners. That would surely show them where his intentions lay.

As the ditch neared the Yankee camp it got more and more shallow, and the rebel prisoners had to step up on exposed ground. They stretched their hands as high above their heads as they could, yelling, "We give up! Don't shoot!"

Several men in blue turned and leveled their rifles at the handful of rebels. Their mouths fell open in awe when they realized the rebel prisoners were being led to them by a contingent of black men, with one pointing a pistol at their backs and four brandishing rifles with fixed bayonets.

"Well I'll be damned," commented a Union sergeant stepping forward from the group. "I never thought I'd be seeing a sight like this."

The sergeant barked back over his shoulder to his men and said, "Boys, take these prisoners over to where we've got the others." Then he stepped over to George and said, "I'm Sergeant Wilson, and I'd like to welcome you to the fightin' Illinois Eleventh Infantry."

George looked down at the sergeant's offered hand. He'd never had a white man offer him his hand in friendship, and he wasn't too sure how to react. The sergeant could see his discomfort, and slid his hand back to his side.

"You boys damn sure wanted your freedom pretty bad," the sergeant said. "Come on now, I got to take you over to the Captain and tell him what you did."

The sergeant turned on his heels and marched toward the Captain's quarters, shaking his head in disbelief, still mumbling to himself, "Never thought I'd see the day."

George and the rest of his group followed along behind the sergeant, taking their first real steps of freedom.

Chapter 7

The Tide Changes

Sergeant Wilson grinned from ear to ear as he extended his hand again to George and all the others of this unusual group. This time everyone gripped his hand and shook it for all it was worth, their faces expressed grins even grander than his.

When handshakes and back-slaps had gone all around, the sergeant tipped his chin toward a tent off in the distance and said, "You men come on with me and let me introduce you to someone that will be thrilled to death to meet you."

Wilson stepped to the front of the group and put his arm around George's shoulder, leading him and his group across the compound.

Before they got all the way to the command tent, the canvas flap flew back and a large red-faced man stepped out into the sun, adjusting his hat on his head and staring at the strange group coming toward him.

Sergeant Wilson immediately stopped in his tracks and snapped a sharp salute and said, "Captain, you aren't going to believe it, but these fellows just brought in four rebel prisoners. I thought it only proper to let you greet them yourself."

The Captain returned Wilson's salute and glanced over the group of men, giving them a quick appraisal. "Glad you boys made it, and I'd like to visit with you, but at the moment I got a real problem that needs tending to. I got men down in that field of battle, and there's a bunch of them in a bad way and need medical attention. I got to get someone out there to bring them in."

Without giving it a second thought, Sergeant Wilson snapped another crisp salute and said, "We'll get it done, sir."

Before he could turn to give the order to his men, George gripped him by the arm and asked, "Could you use a little help?"

Wilson smiled and said, "Damn right. We could use all the help you could give us."

George turned to his group and declared, "You's all free men now; free to make up your own minds. Any of you want to join me?"

Joe was the first to speak up. "I'm comin' with ya', George. The rest of ya' can follow along if ya' wants to."

Every single man fell in behind George and Joe and Sergeant Wilson without a moment's hesitation, just like they were a part of the Fightin' Illinois.

Wilson said, "Men, we are going out there and get those wounded boys and bring 'em in for the care they need and deserve. They are your brothers now, and I know they'd do the same for you. Now, fall to it!"

George and the others were immediately filled with a newfound sense of pride and belonging and took quickly to the work of bringing in the wounded.

After about a couple of hours George stopped for a moment and looked out across the field of battle and said, "I ain't believin' what I'm seein', Joe; there's as many out there needin' us now as they was when we started."

Joe nodded his head in agreement, and then George continued, "I think we need to get high up on that ridge and get some of them fellers up there. They's been hollerin' for help for a long time and we needs to give it to 'em."

Joe said, "Then let's do it." He broke out into a full sprint toward the ridge with George following behind him this time. It was at least a quarter of a mile to the fallen soldiers and they would have to brave much more open field than before, when they had been shielded by the protection of the tree line.

When they got to the ridge they were greeted with a sad finding.

Most of the men were already dead.

The first live soldier they got to was a young lieutenant. He'd been hit in the leg, but had been able to stem the bleeding, but it was so badly broken that he couldn't walk on his own, but he had lost so much blood, he probably could not have walked if he could. For just a brief moment his excruciating pain was secondary, overshadowed by the surprise of seeing that it was two black men that had come to save him.

"I don't know who you are or how you got here, but I been a prayin' to God for help ever since I got hit, so he surely must have sent you," he said in a weak voice.

George and Joe just smiled an acknowledgement, still not completely comfortable with all the kind attention they were getting from these white men.

"You better keep your heads down," the young soldier said. "Those bastards over in those trees have been sniping at us on the ground for over an hour. Most of those dead men you passed getting to me were alive before those bastards did their dirty work."

As George and Joe were bent over tending to the lieutenant, a musket ball made a sound like a hornet as it whizzed between them. They crouched lower and turned to look toward the trees and saw five gray-clad men charging their way with nasty looking bayonets gleaming off the end of their rifles.

"We's gonna butcher you niggers like hogs!" yelled one of the marauders.

George and Joe immediately jumped to their feet, knowing that if they were going to survive now, it was totally up to them.

"If you ever want to see Bess and your kids again, you better be makin' sure you kill those bastards!" George shouted.

Both men grabbed rifles and bayonets from the ground, and turned to face their advocacies.

When the rebs were within thirty feet, a shot rang out and one of them staggered and then fell to the ground. George looked down and saw the lieutenant brandishing his pistol, and thought what a dead-eye shot he was.

The lieutenant looked up and said, "Sorry boys that was my last shot." With a rifel in one hand, George pulled the master's pistol from his belt with the other, and fired. Then he fired again, but not one charging soldier fell. Then he dropped the pistol at the Lieutenant's side and set his feet solid, preparing for the coming onslaught.

The first rebel to reach George wildly thrust his bayonet at his chest, but George turned to the side and responded with a vicious blow to his attacker's head with the butt of his rifle. He then spun and pointed the tip of his new tool toward the next adversary. He faked a high thrust with the bayonet, and when the reb feigned to the left, George thrust again and buried his blade up to the hilt in the man's stomach. George bulled forward, pushing the man until he fell to his back on the ground, dead.

George withdrew the bayonet from the soldier's gut, and then jumped across his body and stormed toward where Joe was fighting off his own attackers. Just as he got near his friend, one of the gray-coats let out a rebel yell, and trusted his bayonet deep into Joe's chest. It was like an unbelievable dream, and George was watching it all happen; helpless to save his friend in time.

George stepped two more steps forward, putting him in range, and he delivered a killing blow to the side of the man's head with the butt of his musket, but not before the rebels blade had pierced Joe's chest.

In the same instant, the lieutenant had turned to his side and fired a round from Winthrop's pistol dropping the last rebel as he was running toward George with his bayonet at the ready.

Joe crumpled to the ground.

George surveyed the dead rebels and then knelt by his friend's side. He gentle lifted his head up off the ground, trying to comfort him. Joe coughed and blood splattered and foamed in his mouth. Both men knew he was mortally wounded.

"Well, I's free...I's finally free," Joe struggled to say. George cradled his head in his hands. "George, ya' gotta tell Bess I left this world a free man. It be important that she know that. And tell her I'll miss her."

Those were the last words Joe said, and then he closed his eyes for the last time.

George gently laid his friend's head down on the ground, and then stood tall and gripped the rifle in his hand. He walked over to the body of the man who'd killed his friend. He knew he was already dead, but he smashed the butt of his weapon against the man's head, again and again.

He was getting final vengeance on the man who'd killed his friend; killed him on the first, and only free day of his life.

Now George went back to the work of saving his new-found brethren. He picked the lieutenant up in his arms and carried him toward the safety of camp. When he got about half way there, two other soldiers met him and took the lieutenant from him.

George followed along behind them; his head down and his thoughts in a haze. He'd just watched his best friend die in his arms, and he'd been in hand-to-hand battles to the death with men he'd never laid eyes on before. It was all like a dream... a horrible nightmare, but he knew it was real.

When they got back to the safety of camp, George flopped down and sat on the ground next to the lieutenant while they waited for a doctor to come tend to him.

"Why didn't you shoot them rebs with your pistol?" the lieutenant asked.

George was staring off into the distance, still lost in the thoughts of all that had happened. "I don't knows how to shoot," he said.

"You mean you never learned how to shoot a pistol?"

"No, I means I never learned how to shoot nothin'," George said. "I only shot a gun one time in my life." George was thinking about when he'd shot the master in the head.

"Well, you damn sure handled that bayonet like a veteran," the lieutenant declared.

"Yeah, I guess I did," George agreed. "Ain't done that before, neither, but I's spent my life usin' tools out in the fields, and after a few lashes, for choppin' down cotton plants, you learn how to make your tool go exactly where you want it."

"Well, maybe you can't shoot, but you can damn sure fight. And by the way, my name is Young; Ed Young." The man lifted up off the ground just a little and extended his hand to George. "I want to thank you for what you did, and if I can ever be of any help to you, all you've got to do is ask."

"Well sir, I'm glad I could help, but I never had any notion that the price of freedom was gonna cost me the life of my best friend, and now that I think about it, I suppose it's gonna cost me my family, too," George lamented.

"I'm sorry for what you lost, my friend, but this war is going to cost a lot of people a lot of things. We just got to hope it's all worth it in the end."

George nodded, still deep in his own thoughts. "What your name?"

"George."

"George what? I want to be sure and remember you."

George thought about that for a moment. "Don't rightly know. I never really had no other name, but they tell me I'm a Goldsby."

"Well, George Goldsby, it's a pleasure to know you." The lieutenant patted his hand on George's leg.

"I'm going to recommend to the Captain that you and your men be transferred to the transportation division. All of you can be a great help in bringing all this fighting to an end. While I'm at it, I'm going to do what I can to see to it that you get corporal stripes, too. I know Sergeant Wilson will back me up on that, so I don't think it will be any problem at all."

George nodded his head, listening to the lieutenant. The reality of all that had happened, and all that was about to happen in his life still hadn't hit home in his mind at this point in time.

Chapter 8

The Struggle Continues

On the heels of the strong recommendations by Lieutenant Young and Sergeant Wilson, George and his group were all transferred to the transportation unit in Harrisburg, Pennsylvania. And it was there where they'd first meet Sergeant O'Malley.

O'Malley was a large red-faced man that had a manner of speaking unlike anything any of them had ever heard, and when they asked about it, they were told that he'd just gotten off the boat from his homeland in Ireland. They also learned that he'd served in the English army, and had been stationed in India for a time. Sergeant O'Malley was an interesting man who was full of English pomp and formality, and fascinated George to no end, as he was the first man he'd ever met who'd seen so much of the world.

O'Malley barked orders to the men like he was speaking for the Lord, and when he spoke it was clear that he expected an immediate and unwavering response. In fact, when George and his companions were first exposed to the Sergeant, it was a little like they were back listening to the demanding dictates of Boss Tucker. However, they quickly learned that Sergeant O'Malley wasn't dictating to them like they were lesser men than he, but that he expected them to carry on like soldiers and do their duty like any other men under his command. They soon learned the difference between being commanded like free men in the military, and being 'owned' like they were before.

O'Malley had the men up at the break of dawn, performing their daily drills, including the proper use of a rifle and bayonet. He'd push the men relentlessly, and then let them rest for five minutes, and then sent them to doing the job at hand, which was loading wagons and train cars with the much needed supplies. It was long, grueling hours of work, but it was a labor with a purpose; this was one of the major supply depots and a fighting man without supplies was useless.

George and the other men were already accustomed to long hard days of work, and they held up well under the combination of work and training. In fact, it was almost like a blessing to them that they no longer had to toil under the unbearable Alabama sun.

One of the greatest surprises to the newly freed men came at the end of their first month in Harrisburg, when they were called to fall in with the rest of the troops to receive their pay. George was the first in line of the Negro troops, and when he got to the paymaster's table he was told to sign his name.

George looked at the stern man seated behind the table and said, "Sir, I don't know how to sign my name, and neither do any of the rest of us."

Without missing a beat, the man said, "Then put an X right here on this line."

George scratched out an X to indicate his name, and for the first time in his life he was handed a stack of twenty coins for the work he'd done. He held those coins in his hand, just staring down at them for the longest time, rolling them over and over and feeling their weight in his hand, and the pride that it gave him.

Finally the paymaster said, "Corporal, you need to move on; there are other men that need to be paid."

After they'd all been paid, George and his cohorts walked over and squatted down in the shade of a big Elm tree.

"What is we gonna do with this? I ain't never seen nothin' like it before," said one of the men.

"Ain't none of us ever seen nothin' like it," George said, "But I know what I's gonna do with it. I's gonna save ever one of these coins so that when this here war is over, I can get back to Alabama and get my wife and kids."

This declaration brought a silence to the gathering, as they all fell into a silence as they revisited their past life.

George looked off to the southern horizon, emptiness etched across his face as he thought about his family; the family he knew was still under the heavy-handed burden of being slaves.

The war lingered on, and along with their daily drills and the decent food and the hard work, the men were not only healthier than they had ever been in their lives, but when they heard of battles being won, they felt like they were truly a part of something important; a part of something as free men.

As time passed they became friends with some of the white soldiers. This was an accomplishment as they were housed separately, but the bravery that they had exhibited on the battle field had caused many a white soldier to accept them.

During the visits with their fellow soldier they learned that they were receiving less money than the white soldiers. They also learned that they were being charged for their uniforms and the others weren't.

This bothered the men to some extent, but then they realized that at least they were free and the work they were doing was not near as hard as that they had performed in the field on the plantation and at least now they were being paid something and fed far better than back home.

One day Sergeant O'Malley came and said, "Men, we have a new assignment. You've trained hard and learned how to be good soldiers, and I know you're ready. We're going to travel on the train on this trip. You're going to be responsible for loading and unloading all along the route, and I've promised the commanding officers that you men can get it done faster and smoother than anybody in this man's army."

George and the men looked at each other and smiled filled with the pride of knowing that they were being respected for their hard work and abilities. They'd loaded and unloaded countless train cars while they were in Harrisburg, and they'd always talked about what an adventure it would be to actually get to travel on one of those steel beasts when they pulled out of the station. They'd always thought it was just a dream, but now it was becoming a reality; a dream come true.

The next morning the train that pulled into the station was strung with more cars that George and any of the others had ever seen at one time. O'Malley said, "Well men, there she is. Now get your backs into it and let's show these ladies how a real men work."

They quickly loaded the first two flatcars with nothing but sacks and sacks of potatoes, and then set about loading the boxcars with crates and boxes of rifles, powder, and shot.

The men were constantly encouraged by O'Malley and his promises that they were doing more than just loading the cars now; they were actually going to be a part of the adventure when it rolled out of the station.

There were twenty-five boxcars and two flatcars, and two passenger cars situated between them. When they had finished loading the last of the freight, the men stood by with great anticipation just waiting for the order to board and start their long dreamed of adventure.

O'Malley stepped up on the platform and ordered, "You men go on down to the creek and bathe, and then go to your quarters and dress in full uniform. After that, pack two changes of clothes and your full fighting gear and report back here in one hour."

The men rushed to their final duties at the base, and then reported back to the platform as instructed. They stood there at proud attention, watching as forty uniformed and fully armed soldiers entered the passenger cars.

"Now, you men are going to take a position in the last boxcar," O'Malley instructed. "You'll stay there until ordered to move out and unload the assigned cars. Corporal Goldsby, you'll be in charge. Now, be quick about it!"

George and the men took their assigned post as ordered, and while they were thrilled to be on board, they questioned why they were relegated to the boxcar. After a little grumbling, they heard the wail of the steam whistle and felt the first jolt as the train lurched forward, and their grumbling stopped and smiles stretched across their faces. The sound of metal clanging as the slack pulled out between the cars was music to their ears. The train was finally pulling out of the station, and they were actually a part of this new and exciting quest.

The train rumbled along the tracks for almost six hours before it pulled to its first stop. The men jumped to their feet and straightened their uniforms, and before they could get themselves to full attention, the sliding door slid open and

O'Malley shouted, "Get over to the fourth and fifth car and fill those wagons with what they've been waiting for!" Show those boys what real soldiers can do!"

While they were hustling supplies out of the boxcars and into the wagons of the waiting men, they all listened to talk about how these soldiers were hurrying to be a part of a movement led by General Sherman. They didn't get all the details, but it was evident that it was something that was going to be massive and critical to the war effort.

When the last crate was unloaded, O'Malley barked, "Corporal Goldsby, tell your men that they did an excellent job! Now, get them back to their car and get some rest while they can. We're scheduled for another big supply stop in about three hours."

George and his men loaded back into their car and were fast asleep in a matter of minutes, they'd worked at breakneck speed and had well-earned the rest.

The train pulled on toward the next stop, and the rocking and clacking of the rails seemed like a lullaby to the slumbering men.

After about an hour and a half, all those sleeping were rudely awakened by the screeching of the brakes and a jolting stop of the train. Then there was an immediate and harsh wail of the engine whistle.

While the men tried to gain their wits about them, the entire western hillside that bordered the track erupted with gunfire. The Confederates were staging a surprise attack against the supply train, and their tactic was working, catching the troops in the passenger cars, completely off-guard.

George slung the boxcar door open, and could look up the line and see round after piercing Confederate round penetrating the two passenger cars. The intensity of the fire made it like they were exploding under the constant barrage of the attack. He immediately took command of the situation and ordered his men, "We got to do somthin' and do it now! Get your fightin' stuff and follow me!"

He cautiously slid back the door on the other side of their car and quickly concluded that there was no attack coming from that direction. He jumped to the ground with his rifle in hand and his men immediately followed suit.

George led the men around the end of the car and watched as the hail of fire continued from the hillside. He could see the Union troops returning fire, but it was evident that they were no match for the sheer numbers of Confederate troops and their superior position. They had planned this attack well, and were taking every advantage.

George motioned for the men to follow him to the tree line on the east side of the track, and they took a secure position as soon as they could; crouched in the cover of the brush.

Now, they had the north flank on the rebels, and evidently still hadn't been noticed since all the attack was concentrated on the two passenger cars.

George assessed the situation for a moment, and then said, "Men, before we do this, I want you to understand, I been told that there ain't no such thing as a colored prisoner of war. If they catch you, they gonna kill you, so you ain't fightin' just to save this train. You is fightin' for your life."

"Now, we's gonna move right down this tree line and attack those rebs with everthin' we got. Find your target and make sure you hit it good. When you fire, reload as fast as you can, and then find another target and hit it. After you fire our second round, we're gonna charge 'em with our bayonets. I want you screaming like you were on fire, let's make those rebs think that the whole army is comin' after 'em. We got to get it done or we be dead men. Fight like you is fightin for your mamma!"

As the men moved forward the thought of Joe's death flashed into George's mind, and he thought about the truth that free men die just as easily as slaves do in battle.

The men followed his orders just as if he had ordered them to hoe another row of cotton. O'Malley's rigid training methods were paying off and they were all deadly accurate with their rifles. After their second shots were fired they all let out a blood curdling cry and bravely attacked the rebel stronghold and in short order had routed the totally surprised aggressors.

When the dust of the battle had settled, George and his men tallied the damage; ten dead and six lay wounded. The wounded that were able were marched to the train with their hands held high over their heads.

George quickly assessed his men and saw that only two had been slightly wounded. He puffed out his chest with pride, and was thrilled that he hadn't lost another friend to battle.

The Captain in charge of the train staggered out of the passenger car; blood soaking through the sleeve of his uniform jacket from a round he'd taken in the shoulder.

"My God, where did you boys come from? If it hadn't been for you and that great flanking maneuver, we'd all surely be dead. How did you figure you needed to attack them from the north?"

George still stood at attention, "Sir, when you is facin' a mad bull, you sure don't want to come at his horn end."

The captain thought for a minute and then a smile came to his face followed by a chuckle. "I wonder why they don't write that in a military manual."

O'Malley stepped from the second passenger car. A huge chunk of his cheek was gone and blood poured down the side of his neck, in spite of him continually mopping at it with his bandana.

Ignoring his injuries, he saluted the men and said, "Captain, these are my men, and I'm damn proud of how well they performed here today. I don't know who it is that's been telling you that Negro's can't fight, but it's pretty damn clear that they don't know what the hell they're talking about."

The Captain nodded his head and looked out over George and his men as they stood proud and kept their bayonets pointed toward their prisoners.

"Well, whoever it is that's spreading those lies in Washington should have been here today. I guarantee they'd be eating those words right about now. I promise that the work these men did today will be in my report."

George, and every man in his charge, stood a little taller and swelled with a little more pride at the Captain's praise.

Chapter 9

New Challenges

The war lingered on and the Negro unit continued with their daily duties in the depot. They worked hard and found great satisfaction in being a part of something so important. However, they did find it a little disheartening to see so many sick and wounded Union soldiers that passed through on almost every train that pulled into the depot. Seeing those suffering men made a great impression on George and his crew, they were witnesses that so many were giving so much for their freedom.

Payday was still the most exciting day in an otherwise mundane routine, and now it was even more poignant since the Negro unit was being paid the same as the rest of the soldiers. The men were assured that this was even more proof that they really were free men.

George had been prudent with his salary and saved over one hundred dollars, and now his newfound wealth brought about a challenge that he never imagined he'd have to deal with. He was afraid that that much money might just be too much of a temptation, even for those that he trusted the most.

So to put his mind at ease, George had found an old rotten tree stump in the woods where he could squirrel away his money. Every payday he'd save back three dollars for his basic needs, and secure the remaining eleven dollars of his salary in the leather pouch he'd secreted away in the old stump.

Every time he'd put a little money in that leather pouch, his thoughts would turn to Alabama, and his burning desire to get back to his wife and children. From all the reports he was hearing from the troops passing through the depot, he knew his real freedom was coming, and he couldn't wait to be back with his family and have a life with them as free citizens.

George walked into the quarters after making his monthly deposit, which now required two pouches and was greeted by Adam and Sam; two men from his unit. They were grinning from ear-to-ear and counting out their money on top of a small table.

Adam looked up and said, "George, this here is gonna go a long ways in starting' us a new life. What's you gonna do with all yours?"

George smiled, thinking about his dreams of his family. "Adam, you know there ain't but one thing on my mind, and that's getting' back to my wife and kids and movin' us all up north. Sergeant O'Malley says there's jobs up in Chicago just a waitin' for good men, and I aim to head up that a way jest as soon as I can. Why, what is you and Sam got on your minds?"

"We ain't got no ties back in the south, so we's plannin' on headin' out to what they callin' the Indian Territory. We seen flyers 'bout that place and they say land is cheap and lots of Negros is goin' there. If it all works out we's gonna have our own city. We's gonna run it like free men and be in control of our own lives for a change."

"Damn, that sounds excitin'," George said, "But is you sure that's possible?"

"Them flyers say it is," Adam declared. "You know I ain't the best at readin', but I had Sergeant O'Malley read it to me and it sure sounded promisin'. Besides, what else can we do? We ain't got nothin' but troubles back in the south, and all this fuss just gives us a hankerin' to be our own men and make our own lives. Come on George, don't that sound excitin' to you too?"

"Freedom." George let the word hang in the air for a minute. "That's the most exciting thing about any of this. But having my Mabel and little Sarah and my boy George bein' with me to enjoy it, well, that just makes it better than cake for me." George's face lit up when he spoke of his wife and children. "Just think, my family ain't never gonna have no boss man lookin' over their shoulders no more, and they ain't never gonna have to fear what might be comin' next. If notin' else comes outta all of this fuss, that makes it all worth fightin' for."

On a cold and harsh day, one that had everyone paying more attention to keeping warm than anything else, a load of crates came through the depot that was filled with pistols and rifles that had been abandoned on the battlefield. One of the crates was dropped and its contents spread across the box car floor.

George and his crew were the only ones working in that boxcar, and immediately George knew that if he was going to get back to the south to get his family, he'd need protection. He'd seen first-hand the headstrong mindset of the rebels, and he knew they wouldn't give up so easy. He knew their hatred for the Negros was bred into their core, and even if the war ended and the south surrendered, that mindset would linger on for a long time to come, and they wouldn't give it up without even more of a fight, war or not.

George carefully picked through the crate of weapons and selected two matching pistols. He slipped them into a towel that he carried to wipe his brow, and he spent the rest of the day hoping that no one noticed him taking the weapons. He was anxious about the theft, but he also knew that vigilance had been more lax since news from the front was that the war was almost over, and now it was more of just a waiting game for the men at the depot.

It had been a particularly harsh winter, and with spring approaching the men's spirits seemed to be lifting. But nothing lifted their spirits as much as that April day when the operator of the telegraph came running out waving a yellow piece of paper and shouting, "Lee has surrendered! Lee has surrendered!"

The men were absolutely jubilant and the elation around the depot was nothing like they'd ever seen before. Men patted each other on the back and shook hands and were throwing their caps in the air and many danced around like they were at a Saturday night hoedown. There was knee-slapping and cheers of joy men that simply dropped to their knees in prayers of thankfulness. And as the good news spread to the surrounding city of Harrisburg there was even more revelry with shouts of joy and church bells ringing and gun shots exalting the victory fired to the heavens.

Even O'Malley, who was a man famous for his stern decorum, joined in and smiled and slapped his leg and walked over to his Negro unit and wrapped his arm around each and every one of the men as he shook their hands in congratulations.

"Well, Gentlemen, your day has come. It's what you've all been waiting for, and may I say, it has been a damn pleasure working with you all."

George moved to the front of the men and said, "Sergeant, may I say for all of us, we appreciate your help and that of all the other Union troops. But you sir, will stick in all of our minds for the rest of our lives. You were the first person in our lives that treated us like real men, and I know you've no undestandin' what that means, but it was most confortin'."

He then stood at full attention and snapped a crisp military salute. Immediately, all the men of the unit followed suit, giving O'Malley the respect they felt he deserved, and in a way they knew would mean the most to him.

O'Malley returned the salute to his men, and in a manner uncommon to him, he smiled. "I thank you all for your service, and I greatly respect the work you have done. It would be my pleasure to work with any of you at any time."

George looked down at the ground, not sure how to react to a white man giving him that much respect. It was an emotion he'd never known.

"Sergeant O'Malley, what is you gonna do now that this thing here is over?" George asked.

"There's always a fight going on somewhere in this world, and if you want to find me, that's the place to start looking."

George smiled and said, "We will wish you well and know that whoever gets you is gettin' one hell of a man."

Time passed quickly for the men after Lee's surrender, and the order came down that the men were to be mustered out, and George began making plans for his departure. He'd thought about taking the train as far south as he could, but he knew that once he got there, it would be hard to find anyone that would sell him a horse and saddle, so he knew he'd be better off buying a horse here and striking out on horseback.

George had carefully saved his money, so he knew he had plenty to get what he needed for his journey.

The day finally came and the men had their release papers in hand.

George was elated, and headed straight for the woods to retrieve his savings. He passed two young boys walking toward the depot. They were taking turns rolling a hoop down the road and giggling about something like young boys tend to do.

One of the young freckle-faced boys looked up at George and said, "Did you hear...Lee has serquinded ?"

George smiled back at the two boys and replied, "Sure did, but that was a while back, but weren't it a great day?"

The boy's grin was even wider. "Yep, sure was. Who is this Lee feller' anyway?"

George laughed. "Young man, from all I know, he was the General for the South, and he was one hell of a fightin' man."

"I figured it must have been sometin' great 'cause them two fellers we say back in the woods was really havin' themselves one big celebration."

"What two fellers?" George's smile faded.

"Hawkins and Taylor, they came a runnin' out of the woods toward town. They's always up to somehtin', but they seemed more excited than usual. We just figured it was because they was celebratin' this Lee thing."

George looked over the boy's shoulders to where they were pointing to the woods, and a cold chill ran down his spine. He broke into a full run toward his stash.

When George got to the old rotted stump, he didn't even have to look into his hiding place to know what had happened. There was one axe lying on the ground and another stuck right in top of his secret place, splitting it wide open.

George spun on his heel and sprinted back to the two boys. "Son, how would you like to make a dollar?"

"A dollar, a whole dollar? I sure would," the boy said excitedly as he shifted from one foot to the other and smiled as if he was ready to consume a hot apple pie.

"Then show me how fast you can run. I want you to run with me into town and point out them two fellers you saw comin' out of the woods."

"For a dollar, mister, I can run like the wind. But there ain't no need to be runnin'. They's gonna be in the saloon, just like they are every day," the boy explained.

"That ain't no never mind to me," George said. "Let's run!"

"You the boss," the boy said, and they took off in a break-neck dash for town.

George hadn't ever been in the saloon, but most of the other men of the unit had and he knew it was a gathering place for many of the troops, so when they reached the swinging doors, he stopped for a moment to catch his breath and gather his thoughts.

"Now son, you look in there and see if you can point out them two fellers."

The boy crouched down and looked under the half-doors, and then rose back up. "Yep, just like I said they'd be, they's there."

"All you gotta do now is point 'em out and I'll give you that dollar," George said.

"It's them two guys standin' at the bar. Hawkins has on the red neckerchief and Taylor is the one standin' right next to 'im."

When George handed the dollar to the one boy, the other said, "I don't know why you want to be messin' with them two fellers. My ma told me to never get around that Hawkins. He done stole some stuff from outta our house and he's always beatin' up on his boy. He's a bad man."

While George was talking to the two boys, Sergeant O'Malley and a group of Union soldiers passed to enter the saloon. They pushing their way through the swinging doors and went inside. They didn't even break stride; just patted George on the back and kept moving toward the lure of good whiskey and a fine celebration.

Then, out of curiosity, O'Malley reached back and grabbed one half of the door before it swung closed behind him and said, "George, what are you doing here? I never saw you here before."

" I gots me a little problem, and I'm just gettin' ready to try and solve it."

O'Malley slapped him on the shoulder and said, "Well, you're just the man that can do it," and let the door swing shut.

"Thanks for your help and hope you boys have some fun," George told they boys, and they bound out into the street chasing their hoop and chattering about all the things they could do with the dollar.

George set his jaw and pushed through the swinging doors and into the festive harmony of the saloon. Glasses clinked and men laughed and boasted of their exploits and barmaids giggled and hands slapped down hard on wooden poker tables. He could see his fellow soldiers huddled around tables on the right-hand wall, and other knots of men scattered around the saloon, filling it to capacity.

George took a deep breath and did what he thought was best; face his problem head-on.

George sauntered right up next to the two men just as they hoisted another shot of whiskey to their lips.

"Excuse me sirs, but you have somethin' that belongs to me, and I'd like it back."

Both men slammed their shot glasses down on the polished wooden bar and simultaneously let out gasps of frustration. They swung around and looked at the intruder.

"You talkin' to us?" Hawkins asked.

"You were cuttin' wood up the road and your found something' in a stump that is mine, and I need it back," George said.

"I got no idea what you're talkin' about," replied Hawkins. "Now, leave us the hell alone," he said as he spun around and showed his back to George.

George just stood there for a minute, and then said, "I'm sorry, but I ain't leavin' 'til I has my money, and I can see it bulgin' in your pockets."

The two men keep their backs to him, and seemed to hesitate for a moment. Finally, Taylor nonchalantly looked back over his shoulder, and out the corner of his mouth said, "You know, us folks has worked our asses off to free you black bastards, and now seems like all we get for our troubles is a bunch of sass."

Taylor and Hawkins clinked glasses and laughed.

"Mister, I ain't tryin' to sass you. All I need is my money so I can get on back to my family."

Taylor said, "We done heard enough of your cryin', so if you want to see your family, I suggest you get the hell on out of here. Truth be, if you ever want to see them again at all, it might be smart that you hit that door pretty damn quick."

George bowed up and stood even taller. "Mister, let me put it like this. I's gonna see my family, and I is gonna do it with what I earned."

Without warning, Hawkins spun around quickly and hit George hard in the chest with the flats of his palms, shoving him back several steps.

"Get the hell out of here or we'll have to kick your black ass!"

"Not happenin'," George said, as he caught his balance and set his feet square and steady.

Hawkins bolted toward him and launched a wild roundhouse punch. George ducked under the attempt and shot out a right hook that caught him solid in the ribs. As Hawkins stumbled, George followed up with a thunderous fist to the side of his head that buckled his knees and dropped him to the floor.

When George turned back from Hawkins, Taylor caught him with a straight right to the face that staggered George back a bit, but it wasn't enough to put him down. George responded by burying a solid left to

Taylor's stomach, knocking the wind completely out of him. George didn't hesitate a second more, hammering a hard fist to the side of Taylor's head, and as he fell forward, George brought up a sharp knee to his face that ended the confrontation, and dumped Taylor next to his buddy Hawkins on the saloon floor.

It had only taken seconds, and George thought it was over. But immediately after Hawkins hit the floor another assailant came charging towards him from the other end of the bar. As George squared himself to ready for the charge, the man slammed face-down on the floor, courtesy of

O'Malley's boot in his path.

Hawkins was beginning to come around and started workings

himself up off the floor.

O'Malley stood up and planted his boot square in the back of the man he'd tripped, and said, "Two to one. I know what my man can do, so that seems like fair odds to me, but that's all there's going to be. Anyone has a problem with that and thinks they want to fight, they'll have to answer to me and my boys." At that, all the soldiers that had come in with O'Malley, kicked back their chairs and stood tall.

Hawkins stepped forward, wiping the blood from his mouth on the sleeve of his shirt. He threw out a crisp left that caught George by surprise and hit him just above his right eye. His head dipped just in time to catch the force of a whistling right.

The two punches buckled George's knees just a bit, but he caught himself before he fell, and sprung up with a powerful uppercut that slammed against Hawkins' chin, driving him backward in an uncontrolled stumble that ended with him flat on his back on the floor; lights out.

But before Hawkins hit the ground, George felt the full weight of Taylor's body slam into him, driving both men into the standing crowd, knocking bystanders in every direction.

George spun around and gripped both hands behind Taylor's neck, yanking his head forward and down, just in time to take the full force of his upward thrust knee. Taylor dropped like a sack of potatoes, out cold.

Now, Hawkins was mumbling incoherently from the floor, trying to regain his senses. George reached down and clamped a vice-like grip to his crotch. The harder George squeezed, the louder Hawkins squealed.

"Give me my money, or I'm gonna show you what real pain is like," George threatened. Every man in the room cringed at the sight and the thought of what Hawkins must be feeling.

Hawkins sputtered in a squeaking voice, and motioned toward his right pocket, "My pocket...it's in my pocket."

George plunged his free hand into the man's pocket and could feel the heft of his leather pouch.

"The rest of it. Where's the rest of it?" George asked. "Or do I just finish bustin' your balls and we call it even?"

Taylor was sitting with his back against the bar now. He'd scooted as far away from George and what he saw him doing to Hawkins as he could. He was instinctively covering his crotch with both hands.

"Hell no, you nigger bastard," as he desperately struggled to get the pouch pulled out of his pocket. He slid it across the floor towards George, and said, "You son-of-a-bitch! You don't fight fair."

George stood up from Hawkins, finally releasing his grip from the man's crotch. He took two steps toward Taylor and snapped a hard kick straight to his face. "That's for sayin' somethin' about my mama," he said, as Taylor slammed back against the bar, and slumped to the floor one last time.

George then turned to Hawkins, who was still setting on the floor and bent forward seeking relief from the pain in his groin. He took two steps forward and fainted a kick to the prone mans groin. When Hawkins placed both hands over his already painful area, George kicked him squarely in the face, sending blood and numerous teeth across the room.

"Now you want a talk fightin' fair, first remember that when a man is desperate he will do anythin' to win, but the kick is for your son, when you want a beat up on someone find someone who's able to defend himself."

George reached up and wiped the blood from his eyebrow, and walked out the door.

You could hear a pin drop in the saloon. No one said a word.

Chapter 10

Heading Home

George strode from the saloon directly to the livery stable. The owner looked up at the man's battered face and said, "Damn, man, you could use some water and a bandage."

"Well, that would be mighty comfortin' right 'bout now, but what I really needs is a horse and a saddle," George said.

"Well then, sit yourself down and I can help you with both."

The man scurried around just outside the door and came back in with a bucket of water and some cloth. While he was tearing the cloth into long strips, George grabbed the bucket and tipped it up, drinking in big gulps like he'd never tasted water before. He sat the bucket back on the floor and splashed water on his face, carefully trying to down some of the swelling.

"Here you go," said the livery owner. "Let me get some horse liniment on them cuts. Gonna' sting like hell, but it'll do you a world of good."

When the salve hit the open wounds George gasped. "Damn, you is right. Feels like you be rubbin' fire on my face."

"No need to worry. I ain't never lost a patient yet," the man chuckled, continuing to tend to George's face.

"I needs me a good travelin' horse," George said, still gritting his teeth at the pain. "I is gonna take a long trip, and I need somethin' that 'ill get me there."

"Well, I got a mare that should do you just fine. Only cost you seventy-five dollars and I'll throw in the saddle. How's that sound?"

"I'll give you sixty-five," said George.

The man rubbed his chin, thinking about the offer. "Tell you what, I'll take seventy, and if I get any closer to what you want we'll have to take turns breathin'," the man said.

"Done," George said.

Buying the horse and saddle had knocked a considerable chunk out of George's savings, but he went on over to the general store and bought himself a new suit of clothes, boots, two extra shirts and trousers.

He mounted his new steed and trotted back toward the quarters. George hadn't really ridden that much in his life, most of his experience had come from riding the mules back from the field after a day's work, and he wasn't entirely comfortable in the saddle, but he figured after he got a few miles under his belt, he'd be fine.

As soon as he got to his bunk, George shed the military garb he'd worn for so long, and put on his new clothes. It felt good and right to be dressed like a citizen now, and he couldn't help himself but to strut around the room a little and enjoy what being a free man really felt like.

After a bit, he put his few belongings in his saddlebags, and rolled his bedroll tight. Then he pried up a floorboard under his bunk and collected his two matching pistols. He rolled them over in his hands a few times, getting the feel. He checked to make sure they were loaded and that the hammers sat on empty chambers. He nodded his head approvingly and slipped them in the saddlebags; one on each side.

George mounted his horse again and rode slowly toward the main gate and the open road. As he got near to the gate, O'Malley was standing in the shade of a huge elm tree. He motioned for George to come near. O'Malley reached his hand up to George, and the two men shook.

O'Malley held the grip a little longer than usual, and looked up at George. "I want to bid you a good farewell, and wish you luck, George. And by God, that was one hell of a fight back there today." O'Malley grinned as he pumped George's hand. While he was locked in this long and heartfelt good-bye he reached into his coat and pulled out a folded piece of paper. He handed it to George and said, "This is a map of the way I think you should go back to Selma. I had the quartermaster draw it for you. It will take you a little longer, but it will send you through the safest areas. There is no telling what you are going to face as you go further south, but hopefully this will keep you out of some trouble. I suggest that you try to find churches and in particular Quaker as you travel. They will help you and send you to others who will help."

"Thank you, sir," George said.

"If you ever need a job, remember that the army can always use good fighting men. I fear that you might not find things back home like you think you will, but I hope you do. I know how much it means to you. But if it doesn't work out, don't forget what I said."

"Thank you for the kind thoughts, sir. And I won't never forget what you said. And I won't never forget you," George said with a little catch in his voice.

It was tough for George to put his heels to the horse's flank, but he knew if he stayed any longer, it would only be harder to leave his friend.

O'Malley was the first white man that George had ever considered a friend. He was the first white man who ever truly showed him respect, and

George knew he was speaking from his heart when he told O'Malley he'd never forget him.

Chapter 11

The Trip

The map that O'Malley had given him was far more useful than George had thought. The terrene was much more rugged than he had anticipated and it would have been extremely easy for him to have gotten lost, but his travels through West Virginia had been surprisingly pleasant. The trails were clear and well used and the rough terrain was completely different than what he was used to seeing back home in Alabama. And so far, all the stops that he needed to make for food and shelter had been friendly experiences. O'Malley's suggestions that he find Quakers had been a real help. It was all like another new adventure. .

The weather in early summer did present several problems. There were days that he couldn't travel at all due to heavy rains, and other times the flooded rivers and creeks were just too dangerous to cross. He could usually fine welcome shelter in someone's barn, or if he needed to, he was usually able to find a cave in the mountains or build a lean-to in the forest, but it slowed his pace, and that just made him even more anxious to get back to his family. He found that when all else failed he could go to a church and get directions to the next point on the map or find food and shelter.

George knew there would be obstacles, and he'd planned for a long, difficult trip. He also believed that the bigger the challenge, the greater the reward, and keeping the thought of holding his wife and children in his arms again fortified him against anything Mother Nature could throw against him.

The deeper he traveled into the south, and the closer he got to his destination, the more hostility he felt focused on him being a black man. It seemed like every day he was stared at, and there were more and more signs that he was venturing into unwelcome territory. So, in order to avoid as much hostility as possible, he traveled mostly at night and tried to seek shelter in old shacks that were occupied by other people of color.

Along the way, George heard from other Black men about the troubles they were still suffering to feed their families. They told him that the old plantation system was gone, and now most of the work that was available back on the plantations was only as sharecroppers. They explained that the new system allowed former slaves to be free from total domination of the masters, but that there was a new type of slavery that no one had expected; a new economic slavery. Sure, they were free men now, but being that they had to provide for their own food and shelter, coupled with borrowing money from the company store for every bit and morsel that they needed, it seemed like their new lives weren't much better than what they'd had in the past.

As George listened to these new tales of woe, it only intensified his concern for his family. Without a man in the house, how were Mabel and the children able to survive? How did they provide for their daily needs? Where were they living? Question after question about his family's wellbeing raced through his already troubled mind. His only consolation was that he knew Mabel was an extremely crafty and resourceful woman, and he could only hope that she could hold the family together until he got back to them.

George had been on the road for over forty days. He knew he was somewhere in Kentucky, and that he still had many more miles to travel.

The good news was that the rains had finally let up. The bad news was that they were replaced with the oppressive heat that he'd almost forgotten about during his time in Pennsylvania.

Just past sunup he heard the piercing, blood-curdling scream of a woman coming from the hillside just above the trail. Then, punctuated by a sound he'd prayed he'd never hear again, the screams came along with the stinging slap of a leather strap striking a human body.

George yanked back on the reigns and halted his horse, looking up in the direction of the unholy sound. He sat motionless for a few moments while visions of his horrific past flashed through his mind.

Suddenly, he saw a small boy running down the hill. There were tears streaming down his reddened face, and as soon as he saw George, he ran directly toward him.

The boy was short of breath from running, and along with his incessant crying he could only spit out his words in emotional and almost incomprehensible bursts.

"Mister, please help. My pa is killin' my ma! Please help her! Please!" he spat and sputtered, looking up to George for salvation.

George instantly reached down and caught the youngster by the arm and pulled him up on the horse.

"Where?" George asked. "Where are they?"

The little fellow pointed up a trail leading through the trees and up the hill. George heeled his mare in the flanks and raced up the trail, holding the small boy in front of him in the saddle.

As soon as he got within sight of the shack he could see the boy's mother lying on the ground and his father standing over her, striking her time and time again across her bare back with the leather strap.

George pulled his horse to a quick stop. With one hand he set the boy on the ground, and with the other he reached into his saddlebag and drew one of his pistols.

As soon as the boy's bare feet hit the ground he was running toward his mother, throwing his little body across her bleeding back, and taking the vicious sting of the next blow of the strap across his own back. He first only grunted and then released a blood curdling wail.

"That's enough!" George yelled, raising his pistol into the air. "That's enough! No more!"

Hearing the warning, the abusive man dropped his arm and held the leather strap at his side, turning to look at the intruder. His whiskered face was as red as fire, and he was winded from the exertion of beating his wife.

"What in the goddamned hell are you doin' on my property?" he screamed at George.

"Your boy asked for my help, and it looks like it was none too soon. What the hell do you think you're a doin'?" George demanded.

The man sneered. "It ain't none of your goddamned business what I's a doin', and if you don't get the hell outa here right now, you is gonna be next!"

The woman was now sitting up, holding her boy in her arms. He continued to scream like he was in mortal pain, and his cries seemed to be the only thing that was taking her mind off of her own horrific injuries.

Her brave actions and motherly love spurred George on even more in her defense.

"Mister, I ain't gonna sit here and watch you treat your wife and son like that no more. It just ain't a gonna happen."

George looked at the lady. "Ma'am, you got a place you can go?"

The woman was too injured to move another inch, and all she could do was mouth a 'no', and shake her head, as tears streamed down her anguished face.

"Is what you tryin' to tell me is that you gotta stay with this bastard?" George asked.

She nodded her head in the affirmative.

"Okay, then," George said. "But I'm damn sure gonna make it so he has one hell of a time chasin' you anymore, and he's gonna need your kindness for his own good."

"What the hell you talkin' about, nigger? I got a good mind to go in the house and get my gun and kill you," the man threatened.

George leveled his pistol at the man and pulled the trigger. The report from the gun echoed in the hills and smoke and fire spat from barrel and a ball struck the man in the center of his foot, dropping him to the ground as he grabbed at his leg and screamed and cursed to the high heavens. He rolled around on the dirt while blood oozed through the toe of his boot and agony etched across his face, the cursing was replaced with moans of pain.

George looked to the woman. She still clutched her son to her chest. Her tears stopped and her face was covered with surprise. Her red eyes opened wide and she looked at her husband rolling around on the ground in pain.

"You shot my husband," she said in utter disbelief.

"Sure did," George said. "And if ya' like, I'll put on in his other foot too."

"No, no, don't hurt him no more," she stammered as she attempted to rise.

"Lady, this man was a beatin' you to death and no one should be a treated that way. I simply fixed it so's he's gonna have a hell of a time doin' it again, and maybe he'll learn that he needs you to take care of 'im now."

George looked back down to the wounded man. "I'll tell you what. Just in case you ain't learned how to treat people, I'll be back by in a few weeks and check on you, and if you ain't learned your lesson, I'll put the next one in your knee. How's about that?"

The man didn't even look up. He just continued to grasp his bleeding foot and roll around on the ground.

"Lady, I'm gonna be on my way now. From time to time you remind that bastard that I might be comin' back. And I truly do hope things is better for you and your boy."

George tipped his hat and kicked his mare in the flanks and disappeared down the trail.

George knew he had to make some distance away from that place, so he traveled more in the day that usual. Luckily, he was able to find some good shelter in a grove of trees several miles away so he could rest. He decided not to build an attention-drawing fire, and settled for only eating hardtack for supper. He figured it better to be safe than sorry, and knew that any attention he drew this close to the shooting, might be the last attention he ever got, and the last time he saw the light of day.

As George settled in for the night, he couldn't believe his good fortune. When he looked up he realized he was bedding down next to a garden, that was just starting to produce. Not only did he eat so much young tinder vegetables that he thought he was going to explode, but his mare was able to share in the unexpected bounty as well.

George was exhausted, and he knew his horse was too, but he felt a little burst of anticipatory energy as he approached the McCain plantation. It had been a long and arduous journey, but now he was more positive than ever that he would soon see Mable and his children, and knowing that they were so close lifted his spirits.

As he traveled up the road to the mansion his nerves were on edge. He wasn't sure how, or even if he'd be welcomed, and his greatest hope at the moment was that dear friend Joseph would still be there.

George had only been here once before, when Miss Daisy had insisted on him driving her there. He remembered it as being a rambling, stately mansion that was more palatial than anything he'd ever seen in the south. Now, it was a mere shell of its former grandeur, having fallen into a state of utter disrepair. What little paint that wasn't sun-faded and dreary, was peeling off like scales on an old fish, and the gardens that had once been filled with carpets of colorful flowers looked like they hadn't known a caring hand in years. Even the grand old moss-covered Live Oak trees that surrounded the home seemed to look sad and dreary.

George approached slowly, hoping that someone would come out and greet him as he came up the road. Then, not seeing a living soul, he was even more uneasy, so he rode on past the house to see if maybe any of the ex-slaves might still be out back near the old quarters.

As he rode past the stable he was shocked to see young Charles McClain come limping out of the wide door with a shotgun in his hand.

"Who in the hell are you and what are you doin' on my property?" McClain demanded.

George immediately raised his hands above his head and said, "I mean you no harm, sir. I am George, from the Winthrop Plantation and I'm looking for Joseph." He slouched a little lower in his saddle, trying to look as unthreatening as possible.

Charles looked at him for a few seconds, and then a little light of recognition flickered in his eyes.

"I know you. You were Winthrop's stud nigger." He lowered his shotgun, but still kept it gripped tightly in his nervous hands. "You went with General Winthrop to the war, and then we heard he got killed at Gettysburg leading something they called Picket's Charge. We were told he died a hero. Were you there with him?"

"Yes, sir, I was there," George said. "And you's right, he died leadin' them fellers right into them Yankee rifles and cannons. It was a hell of a thing to see, and somethin' the south should be damn proud of."

Charles nodded his head, not saying a word, but obviously pleased to hear confirmation of the news.

"What happened to you, sir?" George asked. I heard you went from military school right to the fightin'."

The question caught Charles' attention, and he stood as straight and tall and proud as he could. "Well, I served the glorious south and got my leg blown off when we were trying to stop that bastard Sherman as he was trying to take Atlanta. They sent me home a war hero, and I've been here ever since. I ain't been much good for anything since then, and all I got left is this place, and you can see, it's falling apart. It's one sad time for us 'round here."

"I sure am sorry to hear that, sir, and I truly do hope things gets better for you."

"I appreciate that," Charles said in a sad tone, and then limped over and set down on a bench in front of the stable.

"Is Joseph still around," George asked, still hoping to find his old friend.

Charles just let the question hang in the air for a few moments, cupping his head in his hands and staring down at the peg sticking out of his slack pant leg.

Finally he looked up and said, "He's up at the house. Just go to the back and ask for him."

"Can I leave my horse here, sir?"

"Sure, just put her in a stall and give her some grain. We got to be hospitable to anyone who returned from the war, nigger or not."

George did as he was told, and then quickly walked up the overgrown path toward the back of the house. He could smell the sweet aroma of home cooking as he approached the back door and it reminded him that it had been months since he'd had a real meal; and even longer since he'd had a home-cooked one.

Just as he got to the back door a Negro lady stepped out and slung a pan of water onto the ground. She looked up at George and asked, "Who are you?"

George smiled and said, "I'm George from the Winthrop Plantation. I just got back from the war and I'm a lookin' for Joseph."

"Good Lord," she said, and clapped her hand to the side of her face. "I heard of you and I never figured anyone would ever see any of you boys again."

George just nodded in appreciation.

"If you want to see Joseph, go on out to the garden; he's pickin' some greens. And welcome back."

"Thanks," George said, and quickly spun on his heels and headed to the garden, thrilled that he was about to see his dearest old friend.

As George passed the Live Oak tree he caught his first glimpse of Joseph, and he stood there for just a moment and studied his old friend. Joseph had aged more than George had anticipated. He was much thinner and had a full head of gray hair, and he seemed a little frailer, standing there with an arm-full of greens and carefully reaching down for another batch.

"Joseph," George called out softly.

The man rose up and squinted his eyes, and then shaded his brow with the palm of his hand so he could get a better look against the harsh afternoon sun. Once he saw who it was, he dropped the armful of greens and broke into a full-out run toward his old friend.

Both men opened their arms and embraced each other like brothers. They held their hug for several long moments, only breaking it long enough to pat each other's backs.

"My Lord," Joseph said. I never thought this day would come. I done figured you was either dead or livin' in the north by now. But it is a blessin' to see you all in one piece." He grabbed his old friend again and gave him another brotherly hug, like he was afraid to let him go.

George continued to rock in Joseph's arms while he spoke. "I come all the way from the north to see my family, and there ain't nothin' gonna stop me now. I had to come and see you on the way 'cause you is about as close to family as I know."

The men finally stood back from each other a bit, and George looked into Joseph's eyes. "Damn, it's so good to see a friendly face. I been travelin' for days in some hostile territory and I never knew from one minute to the next what I might be a facin'. So bein' here with you now is more refreshin' than a cool drink on a hot day."

"Come on, George, help me carry them greens up to the house and we can set under that shade tree and talk for as long as the Lord lets us," Joseph said.

The two men walked back over to where Joseph dropped his armful of greens, gathered them back up, and then took the poke up to the waiting ladies at the back door.

Sitting under the shade tree, they just looked at each other for a while, shaking their heads in disbelief. Finally, George spoke first. "You're looking well, Joseph, and I'm glad seein' how long it's been since the last time I seen you. How've things been since I been gone?"

Joseph shook his head, and George could see the sadness in his face. "It's not been good, George. The master had a stroke when he heard that Charles got his leg shot off. I had to care for him night and day for about a month before he died. It was a bad time. And when Charles got here he

had changed so much. He used to be so lively and full of life when he went to military school, but when he come back home, he was just a shell of the man he used to be. He mopes around most of the time and he spends most nights with that old demon rum. He won't make no decisions about what goes on around here and it just seems like he's livin' in some other world in his mind. I try to see that things get done, but it's a real chore. Outside of getting' everybody fed and keepin' their clothes clean, we is just 'bout done here. There is taxes to be paid and I don't know how Charles is gonna get that done. All my people have gone 'cept the house ladies, and there ain't been a seed put in the ground for over a year. Just look around. This place is a mess."

"My God, Joseph, this place used to be such a great plantation. It's just hard to believe what's happened," George proclaimed.

"Yep, it's a sad thing," Joseph said, staring off into the distance, and thinking about what it used to be like.

"How's things at the Winthrop Plantation?" George asked.

"Worse than here. When Mrs. Winthrop heard about the General gettin' killed, she went crazy. And let me tell ya', it didn't help her none at all when Miss Daisy had that little black baby. I done heard that she throw it in the blazin' fireplace and then locked Miss Daisy up in her room for months. Then she sold all her slaves and just set in that rockin' chair of the General's out on the front porch like she was waitin' for her man to come ridin' up at any minute like some ghost from the grave. It was a damn sad thing; that's for sure."

"Wait a minute," George said, caught off guard by what Joseph had said. "She sold all the slaves? When did this happen?"

"It was 'bout a month after she got word that the General got killed. They had a big auction and everythin' was sold off.

"My God, Joseph! Do you know who bought the slaves?" George's mind raced.

"I'm sorry, George. All I gets over here is second-hand news. But from what I heard, they is scattered out all over the south. The price was cheap cause lots of folks knew deep down that the war was gonna be lost, so they knew that whatever they paid for 'em would be lost if they got their freedom."

George leaped to his feet and paced back and forth at the frightful news that he was hearing about what happened to his wife and children; news that they might be scattered all over the south. He nervously rubbed the back of his neck and finally ran both of hands through his hair. There were tears in his eyes and he finally turned back to his friend and asked,

"Joseph, do you got any idea where my family is? Please tell me that you do," George begged. "Please tell me that you do."

Joseph looked down at the ground, ashamed. Then he looked back up at George, with tears in his own eyes. "My friend, I would give the world if I could tell you what you want to know, but that was over two years ago, and I'm afraid they done been scattered to the wind."

"God damn it! God damn it all!" George's voice was a mixture of an angry scream and a tearful cry. He slapped his leg and rubbed both hands over his chest and paced back and forth even more furiously now. He finally dropped to his knees at Joseph's feet and buried his head in his lap.

His chest felt like it was full of hot coals and he gasped for air between mournful cries.

All Joseph could do was rub his hands on his old friend's head and try to console him just a bit, but he knew it wouldn't help.

George's heart was broken.

Chapter 12

The Search

By the time George composed himself it was night, and all he could do was try and get some rest. He'd made up his mind; at dawn he'd be on his way to the Winthrop Plantation, and if there was a God in heaven, surely He would provide a way for him to get a lead on the whereabouts of his family.

By the time the morning sun was breaking the horizon, George was already well on his way to the Winthrop's. He'd bid farewell to Joseph one last time, and turned down the offer of a hot, home-cooked breakfast. There was just too much road to cover and too little time; he needed to find out about his loved ones.

Within an hour he was approaching the road to the Winthrop mansion. He pulled the mare to a slow lope and tried to calm himself. He knew that he had to keep his wits about himself, and that this was probably going to be one of the most trying moments in his life.

George slowed his pace even more as he got closer, not wanting to scare anybody in the house, or start any kind of hostile confrontation.

As he topped the hill he could see a white man walking toward him with a shotgun in his hand. George immediately reined the mare to a slow walk, and held the reins high in his hands so the man could see he was unarmed.

When the man got within thirty feet of him, he raised the shotgun and said, "Stop right where you are. What the hell are you doing here?"

George pulled the horse to a full stop, and calmly said, "I'm George. I used to work here and I went to the war with Master Winthrop. I've come back lookin' for my wife and children."

"Well, get on down off that horse and come here. I've heard of you from Mrs. Winthrop. Let's go on up to the house and see if we can make sure you are who you say you are."

Just as Joseph had said, Mrs. Winthrop was sitting on the porch in the General's old rocker; a shawl around her shoulders, rocking back and forth and staring off into the distance like she was in a world of her own. George hardly recognized her. She used to be such a beautiful and vibrant woman. Now she just looked withered and old and unkempt, like all that was left for her to do was die.

"Madam, this here man says he used to work for you, and that he went to the war with the General."

Mrs. Winthrop just sat there for a few moments, continuing to stare off into the distance.

The men waited.

Finally she turned her head and a smile crept across her face.

"George, thank God you finally got here. I have a great feast ready for my husband. When is he going to get here?"

The two men just listened; both of them saddened at the state Mrs. Winthrop was really in.

"You know, I should have you whipped for not bringing him with you, but I guess he stopped in Selma to buy me something nice and sent you on in to help get things ready for his arrival. It's okay, George, don't worry." She looked back out to the horizon.

The man shook his head and looked at George. "Don't pay her no never mind. She's off in her own little world, and ain't nobody else in there with her."

George didn't have any idea how he was supposed to respond. He was trying to think of something to say, and then the front door swung open and Miss Daisy stepped out onto the porch. At first she seemed startled when she recognized George, and turned like she was going back inside the house. Then she stood her ground and just stared at him.

Miss Daisy didn't look anything like the beautiful, wild-spirited, carefree girl that George had last seen. Her hair was wild and unkempt and her dress was not only simple, but ill-fitting. She had on no makeup and her face looked rough and haggard. She looked like a woman many years older than she actually was, and one that life had been exceptionally hard on.

It seemed like she wanted to say something, so George just stood there and waited. But after a few moments of awkward silence, Daisy just turned and walked back into the house.

"I'm the General's nephew," the man explained. "I try to help with this deplorable mess the best I can, but the burdens of this family is about to get me down. I thought the world of my uncle; I really did. Can you tell me what happened to him?"

George could tell that the man was at the end of his rope. He looked down at the ground, and then back up to the clouds; everywhere he could without having to look into the man's sad eyes. He finally cleared his throat and said, "The master looked grand in his uniform, and when we's got to Gettysburg, he took command of a large group of men. He was brave and fearless and tried to keep the spirits of his men up and ready for what they was about to do. He led the charge and was mowed down like so many of the others. He died like a soldier, and that seemed to be what he wanted. That's really about all I can tell you."

The man just nodded, and his load seemed a little lighter for the moment. "Well, it is a comfort to know he was a hero. You are the first person to be able to tell us what really happened, and I appreciate that. Now, if there is anything I can do to help you, just let me know."

"Sir, I am here for my wife and children. I understand that they was sold some time back and I gotta find 'em. Her name is Mabel and she has a little girl named Sarah and a baby boy named George. Is there anything you can tell me that might help me find 'em?"

"Well, you were told right. All the slaves except the house niggers were sold off at auction. But I might be able to help."

For the first time since he'd heard the horrible news from Joseph, George felt a flicker of hope in his heart.

"After the fighting stopped and Jeff Davis turned us all into second rate citizens, some of the niggers come back. This was their home for a long time, and it was the only place they knew. I think your lady was one of them that I put to share croppin' down by the creek. It does sound a little bit like how you described her and them young'ens."

"How do I get there?" That was all George wanted to know.

"Take the trail there and go about a quarter of a mile to the creek. Turn right and it will be the second shack that you come to."

George grinned from ear to ear. "Well, sir, if you will excuse me, then I gotta get goin'. You got no idea how long I has traveled and how long I been a waitin' for this day."

"God speed to you," the man wished George. "And thank you for them words about my uncle. They do help heal my soul just a little."

George sprinted to the stable and mounted the mare like the barn was on fire. He spun her around and dug his heels into her flanks and she lunged to the trail.

George's mind was filled with the most glorious daydream he'd had in a long time; Mable was standing on the front porch of that shack, with both of their young'ens clinging to her apron and waiting for their daddy to come home.

He covered the distance to the creek in record time, galloping at full speed past the first shack. Then he pulled the mare to a slow walk and collected his thoughts. He wanted to be as calm as he possibly could, but he was about to explode with excitement.

As he neared the shack, he could see a little girl playing out in the yard, and a small boy sitting on the porch.

Then he saw her. Sitting in a chair next to the boy and snapping peas in a wooden bowl, was his Mabel. He almost screamed when he saw her.

George jumped down off the horse and rushed up to the little girl. She looked up and her eyes widened as he reached for her. She screamed, "Mama!" and ran toward the house. At that same moment Mabel stood up and looked out toward the ruckus. She dropped the bowl of peas and scooped her child up in her arms.

Then, the only thing that filled George's mind was the sight of Mabel's hugely swollen belly.

"My God!" Mabel shouted as the little girl looked back at George then suddenly turned and grabbed her mother's neck; hiding her face from this stranger. The little boy began to scream and cry at all the commotion and ran into the shack.

George just stood and stared at the house; at his family, not knowing what to say. George stood in silence trying to gather his thoughts. He felt a pain in his stomach and his chest suddenly felt full and he had to grasp for breath.

Suddenly, a man stepped through the door and out onto the porch. He had little George desperately holding onto his leg and a comforting hand stroking the boy's head.

"What the hell is goin' on out here?" he demanded.

Mable stumbled backward a few steps and sat hard on the chair, still holding her daughter tight against her chest.

"I said, what the hell is goin' on out here?" The man asked again. "This is George." Mable sighed.

"I thought you told me he was dead?" the man said.

George felt like he was living in a nightmare. Everything he'd hoped and prayed for were standing right in front of him. All of his dreams and hopes were close enough for him to reach out and touch. But in the reality of the moment, now he felt like they were a thousand miles away.

Tears streamed down Mabel's face. "I thought he was dead, or if he wasn't, that he'd never come back to this living hell."

Mabel got to her feet and tried to compose herself. "Rufus, take the kids in the house."

Rufus took the boy in his arms and grabbed the little girl's hand. Deep concern etched his face. He stood there for a moment, and then said,

"Come on children', let's give ya' mama a minute to talk to this man."

As they walked through the door, George heard the little girl ask,

"Papa, who is that man?"

Tears welled up in George's eyes. Those were the most hurtful words he'd ever heard.

Mable brushed the front of her dress, and then ran her hand through her hair. She slowly walked to the edge of the porch and grabbed the post as she stepped down on the ground. She hesitantly walked over to George.

She had a smile on her face, but her eyes were filled with confusion and pain.

Finally, she threw her arms around him and said, "George, I don't know what to say. I truly thought you was dead. I don't know what else to say, 'cept that I'm happy that you is alive and that you's here. It's so good to see you, but Rufus and I've been married in the church for quite a spell now and we has a baby boy and another one on the way. I swear, George, none of this would've ever happened if I'd any idea that you was comin' back. I swear that to you."

George pulled Mabel closer to him, holding her like he never wanted to let her go. But the reality of it all began soaking in, and tears flowed down his face, and he could feel Mable gasping for air as she struggle to not break down and lose all control.

Finally, George broke the silence. "Mable, you got no idea how many nights I dreamed of comin' back and bein' with you and the kids. This was gonna be the happiest day of my life. Now, I got no idea what to do. I think I has woke up in hell. I love you with all my heart and have missed you and the kids so much. I just don't know how to take all this in. I'm lost and hurt, and I feel like my world has ended. I just wish I died in the war and didn't have to be seein' this."

"George, I'm so sorry. I missed you greatly for so long, but I had to do somethin' to protect me and your children. I had no choice in the matter. I'm settled here now, and Rufus is a good man and a good papa to the children. He works hard and is tryin' to keep us fed and clothed. I'll always have a place for you in my heart, but this is my life now. I got to stay here and do the best I can to make it right for my husband and children.

"I hope you understand, and I hope you know how hard this is for me."

George gently pushed her back away from him. "I'm tryin' to understand and I'm tryin' to deal with it all, but it's the hardest thing I ever has done."

George just stood and stared at Mable for a long while. Finally he bent over and lovingly kissed her on the forehead and she reached up and wiped the tears from her cheeks. "I guess that sometimes things just don't work out like you hope they would. I don't know nothin' else to do, 'cept tell you that I'll love you and 'em kids, and I always will. I wish you all the best and I hope you have a happy life. Tell my children that I come by, and I'll never forget 'em. I don't know what I'm gonna do, but I'll try to get some-one to write you a letter to tell you where I am. If you ever need me, you just let me know. I'll always be thinkin' of you and my children. That's a promise."

George turned and struggled up on his horse. His body felt like it was stone. "I gotta go. This ain't no place for me to be a hangin' around."

Mable just stood there. Now the torrent of tears let loose and she cried and shuddered, filled with hurt and confusion.

George pulled the reins to the left and spun his horse around. He heeled the mare gently and trotted back up the trail. His eyes were blurred and he never looked back, he couldn't.

Chapter 13

Indian Territory

George was lost. He didn't have a clue where he was going or what he was going to do next. His natural instincts were that he should stay in the area and get reacquainted with his children, but he didn't know how he could do that now.

As he rode up the trail, he decided he'd ask Mrs. Winthrop if maybe she could use a man to help her with the farm or with general work around the mansion; it was obvious that she could certainly use it. He didn't care what the job was. He just felt he had to stay close.

He stopped at the creek to let his horse drink. As the horse drank he slowly stepped deeper and deeper into the gentle flow of the creek. George could feel the cool water against his legs. He slid off his mount and quickly stripped naked, laying his clothes across the saddle so they'd stay dry. Then he waded off further into the river until he was completely submerged. He rubbed his hands through his hair and across his body, and then just stood there, soaking in the water. The refreshing bath helped relax him, but the thoughts of losing all he had dreamed of, kept consuming him.

Naked and alone, this was the first time he actually had a chance to realize how exhausted he really was. He'd traveled for months, and it had been a long, difficult journey, but he'd pushed through, holding on to the dreams he had about how wonderful his life was going to be once he got back to his family. Now those dreams had been crushed to dust. His life was in shambles. He'd put so much faith in his quest for his family, that he'd neglected his own wellbeing. Now he felt the weight of his loneliness.

After nearly an hour of solitude, he changed into some fresh clothes and rode back up to the Winthrop mansion. He dismounted and walked with a renewed purpose, right up onto the front porch.

"Mrs. Winthrop, I'd like to ask you if maybe you could use some help around here?"

Mrs. Winthrop sat silent for a moment, still staring off into the distance, and then replied, "Will you be putting babies in my daughter while you're here? You know she's bad about that."

The response caught George completely off guard. His first instinct was to just turn and leave, but running wasn't in his nature. Her statement caused Daisy and all of her wildness to flash through his mind. These thoughts were then entwined with the frightening sensation that Mrs.

Winthrop might have figured out who the father of Daisy's baby was.

George paused for a moment, trying to gather his thoughts.

"Mrs. Winthrop, I'm sorry to have bothered you. You just go on watch that road and see if the General don't come ridin' back home. In fact, maybe

I'll ride on out myself and see if I can find 'im a comin', and tell 'im he'd better hurry it up because you's a waitin' for 'im."

George nodded a good bye to Mrs. Winthrop and mounted his horse. Without another word, he headed back up the trail. As soon as he was out of sight of the house, he put his heels into the mare's flanks. The only thought on his mind now was to get as far away from that plantation as he possibly could.

His head felt like a nest of snakes; full of confusion. "Damn, did she really know what happened between me and Miss Daisy, or was she just ramblin' on like a crazy old lady?" he said to himself. It didn't really matter now, but all of the chaos, of the day, made him feel like he was carrying the weight of the world on his shoulders.

The only thing George thought he could do for now was to ride back to the McClain plantation. Maybe Joseph could help him make some sense out of everything that had happened, and if nothing else, at least he could get a good night's sleep and fill his belly with a good meal.

As he got closer to the McClain's, he slowed his pace. The sun was setting and he didn't want to startle Charles as long as he was still carrying that old shotgun around, and end up getting shot. "Wouldn't that just be the perfect ending to this a horrible damned day," he said under his breath. Then he thought that might be the perfect ending to the day.

He could see Joseph relaxing under the big Live Oak tree, and as he got closer he hollered out, "Is it okay for me to put my horse in the stable?"

Joseph looked up and nodded, pointing toward the stable.

George stabled the mare, making sure she was well fed and watered. Then he brushed her down and patted her on the neck. "You've served me well. In fact, when I think about it you're about the only good thing I's had on this trip."

Joseph was still lounging under the tree, and as George got closer he stood up and stuck out his hand to greet his old friend. "Did you have any luck?"

George gripped his friend's hand, but it was a weak grasp, and Joseph knew that bad news coming."

"What happened, George?"

George said, "I found 'em, but I lost 'em just as quick."

"What are you telling me?"

"Well, Mable and the kids are alive and well, and livin' back of the Winthrop place. But she's married and has another child, and one in her belly."

Joseph looked down at the ground and absent mindedly kicked his boot in the dirt. He finally looked up and said, "What a hell of a thing to happen. That is terrible news. Hell, it might have been easier on you if you never found 'em."

George thought about it for a minute, and then said, "Yeah, it's a killin' me to think about it, but at least I don't have to wonder about 'em no more. I know they's alive and doin' well. I know they's bein' taken care of, and I guess I can live with knowin' that."

"That's probably a good way of lookin' at it," Joseph agreed.

"I was thinkin' about finding me some work around here," George said. "At least that way I could be close and maybe get to visit them kids some, but I really don't know what to do."

"There ain't no work around here, less you want to sharecrop for someone, and that's just like sellin' yourself back into slavery," Joseph said.

"Maybe goin' back to bein' a slave wouldn't be so bad if I could have my family back."

Joseph looked George square in the eyes. "I know you're a sayin' that, but I know you don't mean it. No matter how bad it gets, sellin' your soul won't provide for nothin' but sorrow in the end, and we's all had enough of that."

Now George stared down at the ground, kicking at the dirt, lost in his thoughts.

"You can stay here for a while, if you want. We can feed you out of the garden, and Charles can use some help with the horses. You can sleep up in the stable and just take it easy for a bit. Maybe a little time will help you figure out what you really want to do."

Joseph finally put his arm around the shoulder of his old friend and said, "Come on, we got some food up at the house. Let's go get us somethin' good to eat. That always helps a man get his wits about 'im."

Things around the McClain plantation worked out better than George had thought they would. He started to feel better about things, and even began putting on a little weight. He was finally getting back to being himself.

Even though Charles straddled the line between being sane and crazy, he was actually pretty pleasant to be around. And to George's surprise, even though most of the horses were little more than standard brood mare stock, there were two that were exceptional animals. One stallion was not only a real beauty, but quite a runner. Charles delighted in watching George ride and put him through his paces.

Early one morning Charles limped out to the stable. He had an unusual little smile on his face, like he was up to something.

"George, they are having a horse race over in Selma next Saturday and the winner gets a hundred dollars. If you want to ride Red Ball, and win, I'll give you ten dollars. I could sure use the money, and I'm sure you wouldn't be too unhappy with a little money, either."

George smiled. "That sure would help me out, and I'll do my damnedest to make it happen."

Both men grinned. Charles limped back up to the house.

The evening before the race, Charles said, "George, go hitch up the wagon and pull it up to the front door at the house. I need you to help me with somethin', and after we get that done we are goin' to Selma for the night.

When George got up to the house, he was surprised to find out that Charles had gathered up all the silver from around the mansion, and was having him load it up into the wagon. To say the least, it was an impressive lot, and George instinctive knew that Charles was taking it all to Selma to sell.

When they finished loading, Charles slung a big tarp over the back of the wagon and then had George help him up into the seat. He handed George the leather reins and said, "Take us to town. We're going to have a great trip tonight and a grand win tomorrow," Charles proclaimed.

Charles smiled and he looked about as happy as George had seen him in a long time.

"Yes, sir," George said.

They traveled slowly along the road because Red Ball was secured and trailing along behind the wagon, and they certainly didn't want to unnecessarily tire him out any more than absolutely necessary.

When they got to town there was a feeling of great celebration in the air, and the first thing they did was take the wagon to the back of a big store. George waited with the wagon and their cargo, and after a while Charles came back out with the storeowner and a helper. All four men lugged several loads of highly polished silver into the back of the store.

When they finished unloading, the owner said, "Well, it's all here, just like you said it'd be." He reached under the counter and handed Charles a hefty leather pouch. "And it's all there, just like I said it'd be."

As they pulled away from the store, Charles reached into the leather pouch and took out two dollars, handing it to George. "Take the wagon and Red

Ball over to the livery, and then find you a place to bed down for the night. The race starts at one tomorrow afternoon, and I want both of you to be ready."

"You sure you want to keep all that money with you?" George asked, looking at Charles and glancing down at the leather pouch. "I could take some of it with me over to the barn. I promise you it'll be safe, and I sure hate to think of you with all that money out here by yourself."

Charles thought about it for a moment, and then said, "You know, my papa liked you, George, and General Winthrop trusted you enough to take you to war with him. This here money is about all we got left, and I aim to take it to the saloon and play poker with it till I get enough to pay all the back taxes on the plantation. But you're right, I don't need it all, and some of it should be saved. Here's two hundred dollars. Guard it with your life. You understand me?"

"Yes, sir," George said. "I do understand, and you'll have this here money right back in your hand, first thing in the mornin'."

George stuffed the money deep in his pocket, and then helped Charles down off the wagon. He went over to the livery and paid the keep for him and the horses for the night. He took great care brushing down Red Ball and making sure he was secure, and then he bedded himself down on a mound of loose hay.

George was exhausted from the trip, and was startled out of a deep sleep when someone punched him in the shoulder. He rolled off the hay and instinctively reached down and gripped the money in his pocket, protecting it. He looked up and saw a strange black face looking down at him.

"Are you George Goldsby?"

George was still shocked at being wakened so abruptly by this stranger.

"How'd you know my name?"

"Listen, I'm a friend, and I've come to warn you that the word is out that you served in the Union Army," the stranger said.

"How in the hell would anybody know that?" George asked.

"I don't know, but if that news gets in the wrong hands, you's a dead nigger. If I was you, I'd be a gettin' my ass outta here."

George was still confused. "How in the hell do you know me, and how do you know all this?"

"One of the fellers you served with in Harrisburg saw you drivin' the wagon in last night. He and some of the rest of us got to drinkin' and he spilled the beans that the two of you was together in the Union Army. Someone overhead him and some Reb boys done snatched him up and took off. I don't know here they was a goin', but I sure wouldn't want to be with 'im."

"Goddamn," George said. "Sounds like I'm in a hell of a fix here. Do you think they know where I am now?"

"I don't think they know you's here in the livery, but I seen you when you was beddin' down your horses, so I come a runnin' when I heard what was a goin' on."

"Jesus, I promised Mr. Charles that I'd wait here for 'im and I don't know what to do now."

"Is your Mr. Charles that McClain boy?"

"Sure is," George said.

"Then you'd better just worry about your own ass, now. Hell will be a freezin' over before he comes to get ya'. I saw him get shot in the saloon last night. They done killed him dead as dirt."

"What?" George couldn't believe what he was hearing.

"Sure thing. There was all kinds of fightin' over some card game, and when he didn't have the money to pay up, some carpetbagger pulled out his pistol and put one right in his brain."

"Jesus Christ! I done woke up in one big nightmare," George lamented.
"You sure has, and if I was you, the only thing this here town would be seein' of me, is my ass gettin' out of here."

George sat for a moment, trying to soak in everything that was happening. He reached under the pile of hay where he'd been sleeping and pulled out the leather pouch. He handed the stranger ten dollars and said, "I don't know who you is, but I think I at least owe you this much for helpin' me like you done."

The stranger waved off the money. You don't owe me nothin', I just figured if you was as brave as they said you was, and risked your life a fightin' in the war to get me my freedom, that this was the least I could do."

"Well I'm a takin' your advice then and gettin' the hell outta here," George said. "Are them streets still full of people?"

"Hell no not now. Everybody is all laid out from all the celebratin' they done last night. But if you's a leavin', you should head out that door and go to the left for two blocks. It's all houses down that way and ain't none of 'em up at this hour. You can ride out to anywhere you want from there."

George quickly saddled up Red Ball and rode out of the livery. He moved off in a slow trot for two blocks, just like the stranger said he should, and then he headed north until he was safely away from town. Then, as he turned west, he was startled by the sight of a man hanging from a tree. The body swung back and forth at the end of the rope; a gruesome pendulum in the light of early morning. George didn't know for sure who the man was, but he felt a sharp stabbing pain of kinship with him. The disgusting sight reminded him of how close he had come to be swinging along with the stranger.

Back when George was still in the army and stationed in Harrisburg, he'd heard some of the troops talk about a place they called Indian Territory. He'd listened to their stories with interest, but never in a million years did the think he'd be heading there himself. That was back when the only thoughts he had were to be with his family again. Now, here he was, getting closer and closer to that strange new place, and the thought of another new adventure actually put his mind at ease.

George didn't really know how many days he'd been riding, or even remember when the last time was that he'd eaten. He just knew that each mile he traveled put him further and further way from his problems and for now, that was good enough.

George had passed someone on the trail that told him Ft. Smith was just a little further on, and that once he crossed the river there he'd be in Indian Territory.

As he rode into town he tried to take careful notice of everything that was going on, and he immediately saw that there were several Negros walking around and going on about their business just like everyone else, like they were free and safe in this new place. He immediately felt more at ease, and for the first time since he'd ridden out of that livery stable back in Selma, he started to relax.

The two hundred dollars he'd held in safekeeping for Charles had turned out to be a godsend. It allowed him to buy grain for his horse and food and shelter for himself along the way, and left him with enough to start his new life here. He didn't have any misgivings about taking the money, because he'd promised to keep it for Charles until the morning of the race, and since Charles had gone and gotten himself killed, George knew he'd kept his word. He'd felt a little sorrow about Charles' fate, but then again, if Charles had really known the truth about what George had done during the war in the fight for freedom, and the fact that he had fathered Daisy's baby their relationship would have been short and unpleasant. George casually followed along behind a small group of Negro women who were walking down the street, their arms full of sacks, looking like they were heading home. Once he felt sure he was in a Negro neighborhood, he slid down off his horse and walked up to the porch of a humble, but well-kept house. It had a nicely painted picket fence and a

flower garden in the front yard that emitted an aroma of sweetness, which gave the yard a welcome and friendly appearance. He slowly walked to the front and knocked on the door.

After peeking through the curtain to see who it was, an attractive dark-skinned lady slightly opened the door.

"Yes, what do you want," she asked.

"I'm truly sorry to bother you, but I'm lookin' for a place where I can get a room and board," George said, respectfully holding his hat in his hand. "I've been on the trail for a long time now, and I'm just lookin' for some peace and quiet. If you could give me some ideas I'd be most thankful."

In spite of his road-weary appearance, his good looks were still evident, and the lady pulled the door open a little wider. "If you got some money, I got some chicken and rice a cookin' that will be ready in about ten minutes. It'll cost you four bits, but there's plenty, and you can eat your fill."

"I got me some money, and I ain't had home-cooked yard bird in over two years. That does sound mighty good," George said, as he smiled at the lovely lady.

"Then go on 'round to the back porch and I'll bring you some warm water to wash up with. By the looks of you, the chicken and rice will be done long before you get cleaned up," she said with a chuckle and a smile.

After he'd washed up, George stepped into the kitchen, still toweling off his wet hair. He was greeted by the kind lady and a Negro man that she immediately introduced as her husband.

While they ate, George told them about having been in the Union Army, and the fact that he'd had to flee Alabama to keep from getting hanged.

The couple listened intently, and with great interest, the more George talked about his exploits, the more relaxed they all became with each other.

They shared stories and the fact that they had all been slaves created a bond. The lady stated that she had been born in the territory and that she was part Cherokee and had received land in the territory that her father now operated as a part of his spread. In the conversation she laughed as she also explained that she also had a little Mexican blood in her, and that might explain why he may have noticed a little spice in his chicken.

After a while the lady spoke up. "My papa is Luge Beck and he lives over in the Territory, close to Fort Gibson. He's got our farm and cattle operation and his hired man just got himself arrested and now he's in the jail here in town. Seems like he was tryin' to make some extra money sellin' whiskey over there and Judge Parker takes a dim view of that. Papa was here yesterday and said it looks like a solid case, so he's gonna be without a hired hand for some time. What I'm gettin' at is, papa needs a good man who can help him out. It's just too big a place for one man to handle and he was wantin' my Henry to come over and help, but he has a little leather shop here and don't want to go."

"I need a job bad," George said. "I know a little bit about cows, and I can ride good, and there ain't nothin' I don't know about farmin'."

"Tell you what I'll do. For two dollars you can stay the night here, out back, and that includes breakfast. And in the mornin', I'll write a letter to my papa and you can carry that to him so he'll know why you're comin'."

"Sounds like a deal," George said excitedly. "But first, I gotta go down to the river and scrub the rest of this road dirt off a me."

"Well, Henry here will take you down around night fall. He needs a good dippin' too," she said, winking at Henry.

George settled in quickly as the new hired hand at the Beck place, and it wasn't long before Ellen, Luges daughter, took note of his good looks, just like her sister had.

Their relationship moved along quickly, and just a few short months after they met, George and Ellen went to Fort Gibson one day and when they returned they told everyone that they were married. Even though their union had all the makings of being a strong one, the working conditions on the farm put a strain on the young newlyweds.

It seemed like there was a continual conflict between George and Luge. No matter what George suggested when it came to the farming operation, Luge immediately and abruptly overruled his ideas. Coupled with the fact that the rains hadn't come nearly as frequently as they needed this season, and the soil just wasn't productive as expected, there were even more disagreements.

Luge was a man set in his ways who had little tolerance for people contradicting his authority. His continual attempts to control and demand obedience from not only George, but all the members of the family reminded George of his days in slavery.

One day the pressure had caused George to take his frustration out on Ellen. He had struck her in the face, after a long argument with Luge. His response to these actions was immediate remorse, but the act had been done and he was at a loss as to how to make up for his hostility.

The lack of income on the farm and the constant family disputes along with having to deal with living in cramped quarters all started to weigh heavy on George, and more and more he started to look forward to his trips into town and away from the family discord.

It was a bright and enjoyable day when he entered Fort Gibson, as he stopped to watch a platoon drilling on the parade grounds. The maneuvers and cadence of the troops, made him think back to how satisfied and fulfilled he'd really felt when he was in the military. As he daydreamed about his past, he suddenly thought he recognized the officer that was overseeing the maneuver, and slowly walked across the grounds to get a closer look.

Sure enough, once he got close enough to see who the man really was, he was face to face with part of his past.

He removed his hat and marched directly to the officer and stuck out his hand in greetings and said, "Sir, do you remember me?'

Captain Ed Young looked at George and a smile immediately crossed his face. He gripped his hand and said, "My God, man, I never would have believed that I'd be running into George Goldsby again. Of course, I remember you. How in the hell could a man forget someone who risked their life to save him?" He pumped George's hand with all the enthusiasm of someone who was truly happy to see an old friend. "I've often wondered what happened to you."

"Well sir, the same goes for me. That day at Gettysburg was a big turnin' point in my life."

"And nearly the end of mine," Young remembered. "What in the hell are you doing in Indian Territory?"

"I'm married to a woman here and I'm workin' on a farm that just barely keeps us fed."

"I'm damn sorry to hear that, but you know, if you want some steady work we could always use you in the Army."

"That does sound mighty appealin' to me," George said. "I spent a couple of years helpin' in the Quartermaster service in Harrisburg, but I got no desire to go back to liftin' and loadin' for a livin'."

"Oh hell no, George, it's nothing like that. They're putting together an all Negro unit up in Kansas, and they're looking for good men with fighting experience. They pay is better and with your ability you'd make rank in no time at all. You can leave your wife here and have money to send home to keep her going. You'll get leave so you can come home and visit, and in some of the places you'd be stationed you can even take her with you.

"They are recruiting men from the north especially around Philadelphia, but they're really looking for good men from anywhere. Can you read and write?"

"My wife has spent a lot of time helpin' me learn to read. We read the good book nearly ever night. I ain't the best, but I can get by. The writin' is somethin' else, but I think I can learn."

"Well, I'll tell you that they sure would take a brave fighting man who could read some, over a raw recruit. I'll send a telegraph to the fort and make sure you can get in, but I'm sure you can."

George stood a little taller and a little straighter, feeling some of his old military training take hold of him.

The Captain continued his sales pitch to George. "They're putting together a cavalry unit right now, and all of the officers have been asked to recommend people that we think fit the bill, and I know you'd be perfect for it. It would be an honor for me to send a letter recommending you."

George wanted to make sure he understood what the Captain was telling him. "You mean I can be in the cavalry and not have to do all that marchin', and at the same time make enough money to send back to take care of my wife?"

"Exactly. What do you think?"

"Well, the farm is only an hour's ride from here, and I'd like to talk it over with Ellen, and I know her papa would be glad to see me go."

"Then mount up and get on out there and talk to you wife, and get back here tomorrow with your answer. I'll have the telegraph reply by this afternoon and I'll go ahead and start writing that letter of recommendation right now," he said with a smile and another pumping handshake.

The next morning, George was back at the fort and was escorted to Captain Young's office. As he entered, Young stood up from behind his desk and asked, "Well, what did you decide?"

"Seems like there's a changin' in my house," George proudly said. "My wife just told me she is gonna have a baby, and we's gonna need some more money to make things meet. She hates to see me go, but it seems like a good way for us to get by. Just one thing I was a wonderin'; can I come home after the baby is born."

"I'm sure you'll be able to see that baby long before it's out of hippen's," the Captain said.

"George scratched his head like he was thinking things over, but the truth was, he'd made up his mind as soon as Captain Young started telling him about the opportunity the day before.

"Well then, where do I sign up?"

Chapter 14

The Tenth Cavalry

It was June and the sun was bright and high in the sky and the wind was blowing. The trip to Fort Leavenworth hadn't been as bad as George guessed it might be. He'd crossed Indian Territory and covered some of the most unbelievable cattle country he'd ever seen. What Alabama had been for crops, Kansas was for grass. He was continually amazed as he rode over miles and miles of rolling hills that were covered with tall grass that in places was as high as his horse's belly.

The only real challenge on the trip so far was that he hadn't seen a single tree, and when the wind whipped up the mid-day heat, a little shade would have been a great relief.

When he rode into the Fort he dismounted and presented his papers and was told to report to Lieutenant Anderson. As he was escorted toward the officer's quarters he was very impressed with the grounds and buildings. His impression of Fort Leavenworth was enhanced by the presence of such a large group of Negros going about their business as if they had a purpose and commitment to something positive.

Lieutenant Anderson was a tall, trim young man. His uniform was well tailored and he had that spit and polish look of a truly dedicated military man.

His office was in strict military order and he stood as George entered. George snapped him a salute and Anderson returned the greeting and said, "At ease, soldier."

Anderson took George's papers and sat back down behind his desk. George stood at attention, a little uneasy, feeling like he was being subject to a strict review.

Anderson read through the letter of recommendation, nodding his head as he considered the details, looking up at George from time to time. The longer he read, the softer his expression became, and finally he smiled.

Well private, looks like I got me a real man here. If these papers are correct and you're anything close to what they say you are, I'd say you should make corporal in no time at all. We'll know for sure as soon as the rest of your records get here.

"Thank you sir," George said, still standing at attention.

"Go on over to the Quartermaster and he will issue you all you need, and also give you a barracks assignment. You'll be in Company F. Get acquainted with the other men and tomorrow we'll see if I've really got what they say they've sent me. Dismissed."

The training was intense and started immediately. The men drilled on horseback. They marched in file and they continually practiced with their Springfield carbines and Colt pistols. The saber drills were the most challenging for George, and while the experienced troops made it look easy, it took some time before he could keep his mount under control while maintaining his balance and hitting his target with the saber. On the other hand, the carbine and pistol practice came much easier to him, and in short order he was qualified with an exceptional score for both weapons.

Colonel Grierson, the Tenth's commanding officer, was a dedicated soldier and treated all of the men and officers in his command with equal respect. The new group of soldiers trained well together,and it wasn't long before they'd become a cohesive fighting unit. Consequently, one afternoon when the Colonel strode out of a meeting with the Fort's commanding officer, the men could immediately sense uneasiness in their leader. This had seemed to be the reaction every time he had met with the Fort commander. However, this time his expression was one of total disgust.

The Colonel called his men to formation. "Gentlemen, return to your quarters and assemble your gear. Anything you can't carry with you is to be delivered to the Quartermaster and will be put in wagons. We have been reassigned to Fort Riley, and we will leave at sun up tomorrow morning. Fort Riley is closer to the assigned lands and being stationed there will make it much easier to fulfill our duties."

Chapter 15

Fort Riley

The Negro troops left Fort Leavenworth at daybreak, with the cavalry units leading the way and the infantry troops marching along behind them. About half way to their destination, the monotony of the trip was suddenly broken by a bugle call to form the Hollow Square drill. While they'd practiced it many times in training, it was still a surprise to have it ordered in the middle of their journey.

As trained, the troops took their positions with quick speed. The infantrymen grouped around the horsemen in columns of three, surrounding the mounted soldiers on all sides. Then the order was given to fix bayonets, and the sound of the men moving in unison had a special rhythm like a locomotive in motion; fluid, strong, and powerful.

When everyone was in position, Captain Armes stepped in front of the men, studying a watch in his hand. "Gentlemen, you took eight minutes and thirty seconds to complete that maneuver. That's not too bad, but we have to be able to perform this maneuver when you least expect it, we'll be ordering this drill again from time to time, and each time you do it, I expect you to knock more time off."

"Yes, sir," the soldiers answered back in one strong voice.

"This formation has been used for hundreds of years, and in most cases it has been undefeatable," the Captain further explained. "And what you must remember is, you infantrymen must not fire until ordered to do so, and that order won't come until the enemy is within one hundred yards."

The men attentively listened to the Captain, soaking in every word, knowing it might be what saved their lives, and what could help them defeat their enemy.

"The reason we have you hold your fire is because once the enemy breaks that one hundred yard mark, all of your shots should be direct hits.

When the smoke clears from that first volley, there should be piles of dead enemy and horses at that distance. The second volley should take out any attackers that survived the first. Many of those remaining will retreat, and when they do, the infantry should break rank and let the mounted men give pursuit. And men, remember this; you will never, and I mean never break rank unless ordered to do so. Then the cavalry will ride down those retreating enemy and deliver the final blow with their carbines and sabers.

"I know most officers don't explain why things are done because they just expect you to do them, but I've found that the better you understand the reason, the better you will perform. I might also add that each of you are responsible for the man on your right, and you will protect him as if your life depends on it, because it does."

"Now, gentlemen, we may never have to use this maneuver in battle, but let me assure you that if we do, it is the most effective way that we know of to save lives in the open field, and Kansas has more open fields than you men can even begin to realize."

That evening after the men had their standard fare of beans, bacon, and hardtack, they all sat around the fire and discussed the day's drill.

They'd done it time and time again back in training, but now with the Captain's explanation, they had a much better picture of why, and what was expected of them.

After one more unexpected call for the Hollow Square drill, the men finally arrived at Fort Riley. They had performed well on their journey, and cut another thirty seconds off the important maneuver.

George had become quick friends with all the cavalrymen of F Company, and had also gotten to know many of the men in other cavalry units. He didn't know as many of the infantry soldiers, but that was mainly because they were housed in different barracks and generally drilled separately.

He received his corporal stripes and took on the authority that came with his new rank. He worked hard at his new role, and part of his responsibility was to get as close to his men as he could in order to build unity among them.

Several of the companies had been sent out to provide protection for a railroad crew that was working about forty miles from Fort Riley. They pitched their camp next to the railroad workers and spent most of their days riding close vigil as the workers went about their business.

One morning, Private John Randall from Company G, was called out and ordered to act as an escort and guide for two hunters who had a letter from a congressman authorizing them to benefit from the services of the soldiers. Randall had experience in the area as he was one of the men who were often sent out to kill antelope or buffalo for the mess.

After Randall and the hunters had been gone from the fort for several hours, George and the others heard numerous shots coming from the west. They knew they weren't shots from the hunting party because they were far too many and far too frequent.

"Mount up!" George ordered. "We've got someone in trouble out there!" The patrol was mounted and at full gallop toward the trouble in short order. As they got closer they could hear the shots were coming even quicker. When they topped a low ridge, the bugler let out the call for 'charge', hoping it would alert the men in distress that help was on the way.

When they got within several hundred yards of the freshly laid railroad track, they could see about fifty Cheyenne warriors scurrying on their horses and making a quick retreat to the west.

George held up his hand and brought his troops to a halt. The shooting had stopped and he saw no reason to lead his men into a possible ambush. It had been a lesson hard learned by some of the patrols that you can't always rely on what you were seeing, this enemy was full of tricks and masters of the ambush. He had his men scatter out as they approached the scene where they'd seen the last smoke from pistol fire.

George motioned for his men to hold their position as he pushed his mount over the raised track. He was astounded when he reached the other side, and turned and signaled for his men to move forward.

There, in a small wash, lay Private Randall. He had a Cheyenne lance sticking out of his back and he was bleeding from nearly every part of his body. He was lying face down; his pistol still gripped in his hand.

George dismounted and rushed toward his fallen comrade. He was certain he was dead before he even got to him. No one could sustain all of those wounds and still be alive.

George reached down and carefully rolled the private over. The man let out a slight sigh. Startled that he was alive, George quickly motioned for the others to come and give aid.

"John, we're here. Relax. You're going to be fine." George knew it was hollow hope, but he was trying to comfort his friend.

Private Randall looked up, blood running from the top of his head and across his face. "Hell, I'm not fine. I got more holes in me than a chicken coop. It's a damned good thing you got here when you did, or I would a had to kill all the rest with my bare hands. That was my last shot," Randall said, forcing a pained grin.

The men worked feverously trying to stop the bleeding, and counted eleven different serious wounds. George sent some of the troops back to camp to get a wagon to transport the private back to the fort.

While some of the men continued to attend to Private Randall, George took the others and searched the area. They found the two hunters about a quarter of a mile from the tracks; dead. They also counted thirteen dead Cheyenne warriors, most of them within pistol range of the dugout.

George shook his head as he returned to the track. "My God, Randall put up one hell of a fight. I just hope and pray that he pulls through. He is damned sure deservin' of any awards that the government wants to give 'im."

When they got him back to the Fort, the doctor did everything possible to patch Randall up, and tried to ease his pain as best he could.

"Think he'll make it, Doc?" George asked.

"He's got more wounds than I care to talk about, but that's the toughest man I have ever worked on. With a little time and a little rest, I think he just might make it."

Amazingly, in a little less than two weeks, Private Randall was up and about, he was still hobbling on one leg and his arm was in a sling, but he was alive and getting better every day.

By the end of the month he was called up in front of the entire Regiment at Fort Riley. Colonel Grierson not only presented him with a letter detailing his deeds signed by General Philip Sheridan, but announced to the entire group that the interpreters that worked with the army had brought word that all of them should be made aware of.

The Colonel said, "The Cheyenne now have a new name for the men of the Colored Companies. They call you "wild buffalos", but I like to thank of you as Buffalo Soldiers. I am told that they use this name with honor and respect. They say among themselves that you men fight like a wounded buffalo, and that you are as strong as a bull, and that your hair is like a buffalo's mane. If you haven't realized it yet, fighting is what they live for, and fighters are what they respect. The buffalo is their life and they hold them in great respect. You men should be proud of this title and wear it well. Additionally, I want you to know that it is an honor to serve as your leader. I have never been around a better group of soldiers.

Chapter 16

Saline River

The tenth was continually on the move. It seemed that no sooner would they encounter hostiles in one place then they would receive an emergency message to rush to another site. By the end of August they had traveled to Fort Hayes.

They had preformed patrols out of this location for two days when a runner came in and told Captain Armes that an entire railroad work party had been massacred about twenty-five miles north of the fort.

He assembled F Company and an infantry unit and they rapidly deployed to the site. They were greeted by an unholy site, when they arrived. The workforce had put up a valiant stand, but they were no match for whatever had attacked them. Their bodies were mutilated as if they had been attacked by mad dogs. They had all been scalped and most had their testacies cut off. Some still had arrows, as many as four sticking from their bodies. It was evident that the attackers had wanted to leave a message that they would give no quarter and would dispense as much pain and mutilation as possible on any that tried to disturb their way of life and invade their ancestral lands.

It was obvious that the force that had struck the work party was large and they had made no attempt to cover their retreat. Armes said, "We've got to pursue them and put an end to this if we can men. Double time and my God be with us."

They moved with as much speed as they could for the tracks were reasonable fresh. They meandered from one flat plan to the creek and river banks. It became evident that the Cheyenne had no fear of what retaliation might be following them. They camped when they wanted and they rested when they wanted.

Armes' men ever found where they had taken time to kill a buffalo and eat it. The small amount of carcass left made it evident that the group was large.

As they continued their pursuit they became aware of a huge cloud of smoke on the horizon. The captain sent Goldsby with a scout party at a rapid pace to investigate.

Goldsby returned in a matter of minutes without the other part of his scout party.

He quickly rode to the captain and said, "They have hit and destroyed some farmers dugout and set his barn on fire. Sir, they have killed and mutilated all there, but we found two little girls that had been hidden in an old dugout down by the creek. I guess it had been prepared just for that purpose. I left the others there to help calm them, but they're in a terrible shape."

Captain Armes ordered a rapid movement to the attack site. When they approached they were met with the usual sight of carnage. The men were scalped and their private parts had been removed and the two women were equally scalped as well and their breast had been unceremoniously removed providing a ghastly and unnerving sight. Even the family dog, a large white creature, had sustained two arrows and lay among his owners.

The two blond girl's blue eyes were red with tears and they were being held by the men of the scouting party, who were frantically attempting to comfort them.

"My God, men cover those bodies now!" commanded Captain Armes. After a few minutes he turned and said. "The infantry will return to FortHayes with the girls. We have to make time. If we don't every settler in this area is going to face this same fate."

As the girls watched their departed kin being placed in the ground one of the girls screamed, "Don't leave Laddie!"Pointing to the dog who still lay in the middle of the blood soaked ground.

Captain Armes rode to her and said, "Little lady, how would it be if we buried him here?"

She looked up at him and wiped the tears from her red and dirty face. "Please, Please do that," then broke into uncontrollable crying as she grabbed her little sister in a comforting embarrass.

With the infantry now returning to the fort the cavalry made good time. They had not seen any more signs of attack on settlers and knew that they were closing on the massive number of hostiles.

On the fourth day the unit came to the Saline River, the right side was a high embankment and the left was gently sloping up into an open plan. It was an amazingly beautiful setting. The wild flowers were in bloom covering the area with a brilliant hue of blue and yellow. The peacefully flowing river and the flowers gave the area the look of as hospitable and as friendly a place as one could wish for. The air was brisk and clean and the aroma of the blooming flowers provided a total contrast to what the men had experienced earlier.

Captain Armes had decided that they needed a well deserved rest and all were pleased that the water was cool and the sun seemed to want to cooperate in their break from the pace.

After a hour of peaceful naps and refreshment Armes put the men back on the trail. They had reached about the center of the open plan when one of the scouts returned riding at full speed. He slid his horse to a stop and fearfully shouted, "Well, Captain it looks like we ain't gonna have to chase these bastards anymore. They is comin' to us. There must be four or five hundred of 'em comin' our way. We best get ready for some real hell!"

Armes immediately had the bugler sound Hollow Square and the men fell to it in rapid time. As they were waiting for the onslaught Armes calmly walked amongst the troops and said, "Gentlemen, we have practiced this time and time again and now is the time to put all your efforts to the test. Every forth man will go to the center and hold the horses. You will hold your position and you will hold your fire until ordered. You will pick your target and you will make it count. Us eighty will put up a fight that the savages have never seen. Because of our numbers we will not pursue the enemy. No sir, we will kill the bastards here as they come to us. Now gentlemen, we are here to fight and fight we will. I ask that God be with us."

As these words were leaving his lips the prairie became alive with Cheyenne warriors. They were close behind the other three scouts that were desperately whipping their mounts with hopes of reaching the safety of the Hollow Square.

The formation brook to allow their entry and the scouts immediately grabbed their carbines and rushed to their defensive position.

When the pursuing hostiles saw the fortification assembled in the middle of the flower covered prairie they halted, and a warrior rode out in front of the enemy and road from one side of the warriors to the other shouting words of strategy or encouragement.

The assemblage was most impressive. Their ponies were a sea of color and their weapons were held in the air. Even at this distance it was obvious that several of them had rifles.

The Cheyenne war chief then rode a few yards out in front a let out a war cry that was followed by as eruption of war cries from his followers.

The savagery and intensity of the cry chilled the trooper's bones as they knew that hell was about to roll down on them.

In a few seconds the mass of aggressors split in two different directions, their ponies at full gallop. When they were a few hundred yards apart they turned and all let out the same blood curdling cry and hoisted their weapons over their heads.

The massive wave came charging toward the defense.

"Captain Armes shouted as the thunderous hoard came toward them. "Hold, Hold!!!! Mark your target."

The riders were now at full speed and within one hundred yards. "Fire", was the next command and the entire front line of kneeling troops sent a volley into the onslaught.

Warriors and ponies fell to the ground, but the war cries continued and the hoard never faltered.

The next order was "Fire," and another Springfield greeting was sent the hostile's way.

More warriors and ponies toppled to the green grass of the prairie. This time the charging mass turned to the right and started to circle the formation. This gave the men on the other side targets and they took advantage of the opportunity to defend themselves and their fellow troopers.

The Cheyenne kept circling and each side of the Hollow Square was able to deliver their blows.

After two complete circles the attackers turned back toward the area they had come from.

Armes immediately shouted, "Men, well done! Replenish your ammunition and get ready. I think they were just testing us."

After a few minutes of calm Armes said, "See that open ground over there about a mile we will mount and rapidly move to that position and reform our defense.

This was accomplished rapidly and no sooner had they set up than another onslaught of attacks commenced. This was repelled with the same efficiency as the first. Despite the immense amount of arrows and a few rifle burst sent their way no one received a wound. However, the Cheyenne left many of their party on the ground.

Armes order another advancement and defensive formation. Just like the previous assault the attackers were repulsed. However, this time one of the troopers was hit by a bullet and died immediately.

Armes ordered, "Strap that trooper over his horse and let's move again. They repeated the previous maneuver slowly working their way toward Fort Hayes.

This time the Indians changed their strategy and came in waves. The change in tactics served them no better than the last except Captain Armes was hit in the leg and as he fell to the ground he shouted. "Keep up the fight men. I'm still with you."

George rushed to his side as he struggled to his feet and provided him with a hand up and a shoulder to steady himself. While there evidently was a expression of pain on the Captains face he never took his eyes off of the hostiles and shouted. "Keep your eyes on the enemy and send these devils to hell!"

The troops kept moving and defending and the attacks from the Cheyenne's kept coming, but the defense proved to be as difficult to penetrate as the Captain had promised. Over a period of eight hours the unit had moved over twenty miles leaving a scattering of Cheyenne bodies ever time they had attack. Finally, the remaining hostiles turned and left the area. They had faced an enemy that had proven too determined and well trained and had lost.

The now weary but triumphant troops finally made it back to the

Fort. They were greeted with cheers by the others and troopers rushed from all corners to lend a hand to their fellow troopers.

As they removed Captain Armes from his mount he said, "Men, I am so proud of your bravery and commitment. You faced odds that should have overrun us and you performed admirably. If we hadn't fought as a unit we would all be scattered across the prairie as our foes are now. It was but with the grace of God that we are now here. I salute you and give him thanks!"

The patrols continued and there were continual contacts with the Indians of the area, but never to the degree that F Company had faced. George received his sergeants strip and thing started to become routine.

One day, as the chill of winter was starting to make life even more uncomfortable, George was granted leave. He was more than excited to be going home. He had received word that Ellen had brought a new little girl into the world and had named her Georgia and he could hardly wait until he reached home.

George's arrival was greeted by Ellen with great excitement and while they were delighted to see each other, George spent as much time as he could with his new little daughter. While he had fathered many children he had made up his mind that this child was going to be the center of his life.

She was beautiful, her brown eyes danced and she seemed to always have a smile. Her raven black hair shined and her light cream skin was so soft and smooth that George could not help but stroke it any time he held her.

What George concluded was that this beautiful baby was the combination of all that she had inherited. Her mother was Negro, Cherokee, and Mexican, while he was white and Negro. He swore that every lovely trait from each race was captured in this one little bundle of joy.

When it became time for him to return to duty it was one of the sadder days of his life.

He felt that he had lost too much family in the past and had no desire to be separated again. It soon however, came to his realization that his work in the army was now providing his family with a secure income and that he really loved the excitement and challenge that the army provided him.

Before he left he made up his mind that this separation would not work. He knew that there were women working for the fort in the laundry and as seamstress's so he loaded his wife and child and took them back to the fort. This gamble worked out, as Ellen was soon a part of the civilian work force.

After his return to the Fort Hays he and the rest of the troopers were on constant patrol. They continually had skirmishes with the Cheyenne and Arapaho that seemed to grow more intent in their demonstration of their contempt on any settler, trapper, freight hauler or railroad worker they could find.

In March, F Company had been called on to run down and eliminate a band of over one hundred members of a combined Cheyenne and Arapaho war party, who had just wiped out a wagon trail of about ten wagons carrying people who were hopeful that there new lands would provide them with a new life. All the new lands had provided them with was a place to rest in peace.

The tracks of the savages were not hard to find and the troops moved with great haste to bring about the end to the merchants of death and mutilation.

The disturbing thing about this effort was that it was now evident that the Indians had acquired an impressive amount of rifles and ammunition.

Over the past few years each time they had defeated new targets they had gained more firepower. Now it looked like they were killing more people from longer range, but were still using their brutal tomahawks, war clubs and knives at close range, to butcher their victims.

The scouts reported back that the war party was camped on a branch of the Republican River just a few miles ahead and the unit hoped to catch them before they were up and moving on this brisk early spring morning.

As they rode down on the camp in at full gallop they found that the Indians had not been nearly as haphazard as they had thought. While most of the warriors were still in camp they must have known that the scout had spotted them and were fully battle ready for the onslaught of troopers.

The next surprise that greeted the company was that a contingent of about thirty warriors lay in wait and as the troops passed, they delivered devastating borage of fire into the right side of the charging troops. Ten troopers were either killed or their horses felled, among them was Sergeant

Goldsby.

Goldsby tried with all his might to hold his horses head up and keep his balance, but it was to no avail. His horse stumbled and then turned to his side and slid to a stop on the tall prairie grass.

George was thrown forward and had done a complete summersault as he had hit the ground. He immediately gained his footing and looked at the other members of his unit who were now entering the campgrounds and being engaged by the prepared warriors.

He turned to see that the thirty who had ambushed his party now were mounted and riding straight at him.

He franticly searched the ground for his Springfield, which had been forced from his hand in the fall and at the same time looked to see what fellow troopers remained to assist in the fight. There were only two other troopers on their feet. The others were badly wounded, struggling to get dislodged from their fallen horse, or dead.

George rapidly shouldered his located rifle and picked the most advanced rider, he quickly sighted in and dislodged the rider from his horse. He then reloaded as he rapidly made his way to his fallen horse and took cover behind the downed animal. He quickly found another target and dispatched him from his pony.

While he was reaching for his colt he shouted to the others, to come and join him in his animal devised fortress. The two slid in behind his horse and both fired their rifles with accuracy. This gave George time to reload his rifle and he took aim at a rider that was less than twenty feet from the fortress and he squeezed the trigger. The rider looked as if he was caught in mid air as his horse ran out from under him and instinctive jumped the dead horse that the men were secured behind.

George ducked as the horse went over his head and saw the handle of his saber directly below him. He clutched it and pulled it free. His companions were now loading their rifles and delivering fire as rapidly as possible.

George suddenly transformed into a man with no recognition of impending death, he stood and with his pistol in his right hand and the saber in his left casually walked around the head of his fallen horse and directly into the remaining charging hostiles. He raised his pistol and fired each time a rider got close, while arrows and bullets passed within inches of his body. On the sixth pull he got nothing put a click. He instantly switched his saber to his right hand and stood for the next attacking rider.

The warrior came at full gallop. Just as he neared the now defiant trooper, George removed his hat and threw it into the oncoming pony's face the pony reacted by veering right and George rapidly spun completely around on his left foot. The yelping hostile tried to stay on his mount and swing his war club, but the unexpected direction change of his pony had made him lose his balance. Before he could collect himself and deliver his fatal blow George thrust his saber into the mounted man's side just below his ribs. The force of the charging pony and Georges thrust pushed the cold steel to the hilt. For an instant the savage was impaled in mid air. When he hit the ground George placed a foot on the warrior's chest and with one pull removed the blood coated saber.

He turned and saw one of his troopers still struggling to release his trapped leg from under his fallen mount; he had his pistol in his hand, but was preoccupied with freeing himself from his exposed position. George rushed to him and with is hand extended shouted, "Give me your pistol!"

The trooper obliged, but before George could turn another warrior had his pony in full stride with his lance pointed directly at his back. A

Springfield report from one of his fellow troopers delivered a killing projectile and the warrior fell from his mount and slid to a stop at George's feet.

George spun around and looked for another target, but the decimated attack party was in full retreat.

Captain Armes announced as he stood in front of the men of F Company. "On this day June, 10th 1868 I hereby promote you to Sergeant Major, in recognition of your outstanding leadership and exemplary bravery." He then extended his hand and a proud smile encompassed his face.

This was followed by with a cheer from the men of F Company. George proudly took the congratulations from his comrades and they all shared in celebrating by breaking out a cask of whiskey which had been ferreted away for such an occasion.

His new position now afforded him more pay and more assistance for his wife and daughter Georgia. This made him feel like he was doing all he could for his family, while at the same time doing something that he had learned to enjoy.

Ellen was as proud of him as if she had received the promotion and showed her feelings with a tremendous amount of hugs and kisses which was followed by a tremendous night of love making.

Chapter 17

Fight for Life

Fort Hays was his home and he had learned that the military was his life. He enjoyed the feeling of authority and the responsibility he now had. His men seemed to like and respect him. He was strict and demanded discipline, but George always strived to be fair and consistent in his dealings. The August morning drill was extra uncomfortable, due to the unusual blistering sun. Sergeant Goldsby and some of his men were standing in the shade of the block house, about the only shade there was in the fort on the plains, when a contingent of troops arrived. They were greeted by the commanding officer and the Colonel was ushered into the Commanders office.

In about half an hour a corporal came from the office and walked directly to George. "Sergeant, they want to see you over at the office."

George had no idea what could be in store for him as he straightened his hat and attempted to brush any dust from his uniform. He entered and immediately saluted the officers gathered there.

"Sergeant, this is Colonel Forsyth and he has made a request that you may find interesting. He is putting together a small group of volunteers that will travel free and rapidly, they will live off of the land and fight like the enemy with no military restraints. Their goal is to attack and destroy any and all savages that they encounter. We are not going to call these men soldiers, they will be known as scouts. He wants men that are fighters and knowledgeable about the territory and the enemy. I have told him that you are a man that fits his needs. If you join him you will still hold your rank and pay, plus you will be doing a great service to the army and your country."

George stood silent for several minutes.

"Now understand that if you don't want to join the Colonel it is fine with me. I sure can use you here at the fort."

"George said, "It sounds like something' I'd like to do, sir."

Colonel Forsyth stepped forward and stuck out his hand. "I'm pleased to have you on board. We will be leaving in about two days. I have a few more men to recruit.

The September days were now turning more brisk and the small unit moved fast and with great intensity. They headed north and were continually searching for signs of their prey, but were having no luck.

George was pleased to be a part of this operation, but felt somewhat out of place. He was the only Negro in the unit and it seemed a little strange. He had always had white officers to answer too, but he was always with a majority of Negros. His uneasiness was soon overcome when he realized that most of the men seemed to accept him as an equal, especially when they learned of his fighting record.

As they road George from time to time looked down at his new Spencer repeating rifle. He was impressed with it and realized that these fifty men carried as much firepower as a full company of men. He could see that this group was designed to be fast and equipped with the most powerful weapons available. The history of the men in the unit also revealed that they were experienced and accomplished fighters. There was no doubt that the group had been assembled to deliver a devastating blow to the savages.

No contact with the enemy was starting to become a concern to all the men. They were all anxious to rid the area of their enemy and they had come to fight. In hopes of making contact, they group turned west and headed toward Fort Wallace.

The fort was a welcome site as the men had pushed hard they had covered more than one hundred miles, and the horses were tired, just like the men. They pitched camp and hoped that word would soon come that would provide them the action they had volunteered to do.

On the morning of September the tenth Lieutenant Beecher called the scouts in and said, "Gentlemen, we've finally got the news we've been hoping for. There's been an attack on a freighter about thirteen miles east of here. Be ready to ride immediately."

They covered the distance in short order. When they arrived they found the usual dead and mutilated bodies. The experienced men of the group quickly summarized that the attack had been carried out by about twenty-five warriors and they had left a trail indicating that they had no fear of reprisal.

The men quickly mounted and feel into rapid pursuit. As the trail continued the tracks constantly indicated that the original twenty-five were joined by more and more ponies. This fact did not deter the pursuers. They had come to fight and this was the opportunity they had been wanting for.

As dusk approached the scouts came to a river and the Colonel ordered Lieutenant Beecher to have the men pitch camp for the evening.

It was a peaceful spot. The river was rolling and the abundance of trees provided plenty of firewood for the comfort from the fall air.

At daybreak, Colonel Forsyth saw the silhouette of an Indian outlined by the freshly rising sun. He never hesitated and put his new Spencer to his shoulder and fired. The Indian dropped dead in his tracks.

The report brought all the men to action. The first thing they noticed was that a group of warriors were trying to release the tethered horses. George and two other men put their Spencers to good use and three invaders fell while the others scattered back into the trees leading only the pack mules.

Forsyth immediately ordered the men to mount and he looked for an escape exit. There was none available. The river was on one side and the trees showed that they had turned into a bee hive of activity, with warriors moving through them in mass.

He shouted, "To the river men!"

George quickly saddled and mounted he pushed his horse and applied his whip forcing him into the river. The water was cold as it encompassed his legs, but he kept applying his boots to the flank and made it across the chest deep river to a sand bar where Forsyth, Beecher and the other were starting to fall into a defensive posture behind a few logs that had been deposited on the island during the rainy season.

It was soon evident that the surprise attack was not by a mere raiding party. The bank from where the scouts had just fled was now covered with

Indians. Colonel Forsyth immediately ordered the men to circle the horses, and to shot them where they stood. As the troopers were doing this the first wave of screaming hostiles hit the rumbling river and started their attack.

George pulled his horse into the circle and pulled his Colt. He placed it to the horses head and pulled the trigger. His mount crumbled to the ground as the report from the other scouts pistols propelled their animals into a circle.

The war cries of the attackers were completely drowned out by the execution of the horses and this was followed by the rapid cracks of the

Spencer rifles. The speed and accuracy of the scouts rifles was totally unexpected by the war party and those who had been the first to attempt to cross the river paid with their lives.

Now the river turned a shade of red as the water started to carry the dead and dying men and their horses downstream. A few unmanned horses floundered in the river for a while and then turned and made their way back to the bank from where they had started.

George took a position behind the carcass of his horse and placed his Spencer in the ready across his now silent body. The scout group was ready for the next attack. George looked to his right and said, "Steve, you got any idea how many are out there?"

"No, but there is way more than there should be, we're gonna have to thin 'em out. A slight smile came across his withered face.

"Well, let's start doin' it." George squeezed the trigger and a hostile, who was crawling up the bank, after having been swept down the river, spun and reentered his watery grave.

"Is that kinda how you think we should do it?" Steve chuckled, "Exactly."

Their moment of lightheartedness was quickly changed when another charge of screaming warriors came down the river toward the other side of the carcass barricade. The Indians had found a place where they could attack without the deep water up the river and they were coming in large numbers. They were firing rifles and sending arrows in torrents.

An arrow struck Georges horse just beside his head as he turned to see the onslaught. He raised his rifle and sent a galloping warrior splashing into the shallow river. All the scouts now were delivering fire at the large party and several warriors and their horses tumbled and rolled to the ground and into the river. A few of the Indians got within thirty feet of

the fortress, but none got any closer as they had all they wanted of the firepower offered up by the experienced and well armed scouts.

The savages that were left on horse turned and retreated up the river.

George looked around the group of scouts and the first thing he say was a group of men huddled around Lieutenant Beecher. He has taken an arrow to his chest and Dr. Moores, the surgeon, was desperately trying to render him aid. In a very short time he stood and shook his head, then turned and walked over toward another scout that he received a wound in his shoulder.

Steve said, "Damn looks like we lost the Lieutenant, sure was a good man."

George said as he shook his head, "Can't be loosin' men now. There's too many Indians and not enough of us to go around."

Steve said, "I been in to many of these to not know that you had better keep shootin' as long as you can and that the lack of them attackin' right now only means that they is up to something' bigger and badder." He reached into his pocket and pulled out a plug of tobacco. He calmly cut a piece off and slipped it into his mouth. He then extended it to George. "You want a chew? Might as well enjoy yourself never know when it'll be your last."

George nodded his head and said, "Thanks."

The lull in the fighting was soon broken when thunderous screams and shouts came tumbling down the river. All the scouts immediately turned toward the commotion. There riding back and forth on a beautiful paint pony was a warrior in a long flowing head dress. He was in front of the throng and was waving his rifle in the air and shouting at the top of his voice as he pumped the rifle up and down in the air, his pony raced from one side of the gathering warriors to the other. The more animated he became the greater the cheers, shouts and blood curdling war cries came from the on looking warriors.

Steve pulled his rifle up in front of him and rested his back on his fallen horse. He looked at the antics for some time and then sent a ball of brown spit to the ground.

"That be old Roman Nose himself. Workin' 'em bastards into a state. Seen 'im before and really never cared to see him again, unless it was in my sights." He sent another brown projectile this time bigger and further. "Yep, killed my wife and kids that time over near the Nebraska territory."

George said, "Maybe the second time is charm. Maybe you'll get a chance to even the score."

"Sure would make my day."

One of the scouts was carrying a basket and in a crouched position came down the line and handed each man two hardtack biscuits. "Better make 'em last or pray this thing don't go on long, 'cause this is the last of 'em. Lost all the rest when we fled camp."

George reached up into his saddle bag and pulled out a slice of jerky. He broke it in half and handed part to Steve. "We ain't hurtin' yet. Enjoy."

The scouts had been on the island all day and shortly before the sun started down Roman Noses' goading evidently had worked because another blistering charge came rapidly down the river. They were met again by the bark of the Spensers and the results were about the same. Except this time more of the scouts sustained wounds. Only one was hit mortally, but at least five were now in need of the doc's care.

Unfortunately, Forsyth was one of those hit. His leg was bleeding profusely and the doc worked rapidly on him. He said, "I can get this blood stopped but the bullet hit the bone and your leg is broken."

Forsyth called some of the men to him that had been with him the longest. "Men we are in a fix here. Someone is going to have to go back to

Fort Wallace and get some help. I know it is a long ways and getting out of this place is going to be a chore, but if someone doesn't get through we are all going to die here. Their numbers will keep coming at us until we are all dead or out of ammunition and either way we're all goners."

While this was happening Steve stood and walked across the breastworks. He had an intent look on his face and he lay down next to the most out laying horse in the fortress. He placed his rifle very calmly over the shoulder of the dead horse. He slowly elevated his sights on the Spenser and stared into the tree branches that lined the bank. He studied the movement of the leaves that were still clinging to the branches. He then rolled over on his stomach and pulled the rifle butt to his shoulder.

George was taking all of this in and wondering what was going through Steve's mind. There was nothing that he could see down the river and the sun was setting so even if there was a target it would have been nearly impossible to make out. He walked over next to where Forsyth was still talking to his men and pickup up his spyglass. He walked to the center of the fortress and looked in the direction that Steve was so obviously concentrating on.

But Steve lay still. After a few minutes Steve's foot moved a few inches to his right and his toe seemed to work itself into the sand. It looked as if you could see Steve's chest expand as his entire body seemed to swell. It slowly started to fall as he exhaled. Then the Spencer spoke.

The lone shot startled most of the men and they immediately turned and were at the ready for another attack.

Far down the river you could hear shouts and just were the bend in the river started you could see franticly moving warriors pulling something from the water and rushing toward the shore.

Steve slowly rose from his position and said, "I got the son-of-a-bitch."

A scout standing said "What did you get?" "I got that son-of-a-bitch Roman Nose." "What the hell are you talking about?"

"I had hoped and prayed this day would come and now I don't give a god damned if I get killed here on this pile of sand. I got him and I know I did. He marked himself with that damned bunch of feathers and he offered me a chance." Steve turned his head to the side and sent out another projectile of brown juice. "I'm tellin' you I hit him dead solid, and he'll die for all the pain and misery he has caused the people of this land and especially, me and my family."

When Steve turned to George he still held the spyglass to his eye, but even in the shadow that it cast on his face you could see a smile that got larger the longer he stood there. George finally pulled the glass down and slowly pushed the ends together.

"Steve, I don't believe what I just saw. I don't know that you killed the bastard, but I can swear that you put one in 'im somewhere."

"Steve's face now was covered with the same smile and he simply said, "I told you so, and the bastard will die."

The scout that had first challenged the shot looked bewildered and he turned to George and said, "You sure you saw it?"

George said, "I damn sure saw 'im fall. I don't know how bad he got hit, but I sure saw 'im fall."

Now most of the scouts were on their feet and they walked to Steve. Some shook his hand, but most patted him on the back and the thought of Roman Nose possibly being dead lifted the men's spirits like no other news could, except seeing a cloud of dust coming over the hills full of a relief column.

One of the scouts said, "Well, if you hit him I'd bet you can't never make that shot again."

Steve looked at him and a smile came to his face, "Want have to." Before the sun rose Jack Stilwell, who everybody had thought was to young and inexperienced to even be a part of this scout party and Pierre Trudeau left camp on their bellies. They crawled to the edge of the water and dog paddled to the far bank. The hesitated there and were soon out of the water and crawling out of sight.

George turned to Steve and said, "Well, I sure hope they make it. They were sure blessed that the moon ain't out. It must be seventy miles back to Fort Wallace. They sure have took on a hell of a load."

Steve said, "Me too, but if they don't I will die right here satisfied."

George turned and noticed that a large chunk of his horse's rump was missing. "What in the hell happened here?"

Steve smiled as he lifted a huge hand full of red raw meat to his mouth and took a bit and twisted it in his mouth while blood ran down his chin, until he had broken the morsel free. "If we ain't got no food we is gonna have to eat what we brought." He lifted the meat to his mouth and took another chomp and handed it to George.

George looked at it as blood ran between his fingers. He finally lifted it to his mouth and duplicated the moves that Steve had made.

The next day was similar to the first, except that before the charge came, the camp received rifle fire from the shore line. In order to protect themselves the scouts had to dig holes in the sand with their hands, because the snipers were on higher ground and able to shot down on them across the horse fortification. While the Indians marksman ship was not great they were able to wound several more of the scouts and while Doctor Mooers was working on one a bullet struck him in the head. He fell forward and never moved a muscle.

After they repelled the charge that followed the sniping, all of the men dug deeper holes. It looked now like it was going to be the scouts trying to locate the snipers and return the favor or the snipers were going to keep on until they found their mark.

When George looked at the scouts in the daylight he started to realize that there wasn't but about five who had not received some sort of wound.

He figured at this pace the little island was going to be the burial grounds for all that were there. Forsyth was still trying to do his job and keep the men motivated and alive. He hobbled from place to place and told the men that they had to hold out for a while longer, that help was on its way. In the afternoon while he was making his speech of encouragement a shot came from the grass and the bullet passed across his forehead. He fell to the ground and let out a cry of pain. He grasps his head as blood flowed across this face and at the same time was trying to reach for his leg that now was so swollen that he had to slit his pants. Most of the men could not understand how he even attempted to move around on it.

By that afternoon the sun had taken its toll on the scout's food source. The odor from the fallen horses permeated the air and the swollen bodies looked as if they were going to explode. In order to keep that from happening they had to slit the bellies open. When this was accomplished the odor became so rancid that most of the men lost what little of the horse meat they had consumed.

If the odor was not enough a torrent of the black flies were coming in swarms. They moved from body to body and never hesitated to stop and take their delight in trying to fly up a scout's nose or attack his eyes and mouth.

Forsyth had a huge blood soaked bandage around his head and the flies apparently thought that this was desert. They continually swarmed him and combined with the pain, the men knew that it wouldn't be long before he parted way with them.

In his condition he was still able to send another two man party out that night to see if they could get to Fort Wallace. He had no idea whether the first group made it and he only knew that time was quickly running out and he had to do anything he could to save his men.

The scouts had proved that they were the superior in frontal combat, so the Indians turned more of their attention to the sniping tactics that were driving the men crazy, when you combined it with no food, except putrid horse meat, the never relenting flies and the odor which now had become so bad that the Indians had starting to suffer. In fact, the troopers noticed that the sniper positions could be predicted by the direction the wind was blowing.

On the morning of the twenty-sixth of September, nine days after this hell had begun George and the men noticed that the incessant gun fire from the grass and high banks did not come. It was a still that confused the men. They were so accustomed to the unholy combination that was tormenting them, that they knew it either meant that the Indians were preparing for their final charge or they were in retreat. The men hoped that it was the latter, but prepared for the charge. Each man struggled to get their emaciated bodies into position and waited.

At about ten in the morning they heard the sweetest sound they had ever heard as the bugle sounded from the approaching relief column.

The men stood and looked in the direction of the beautiful music and smiles started to come to their gaunt, unshaven faces. Those that could move rushed to the river and plunged in hoping to wash some of the stench from their bodies. Those who couldn't struggled to get next to one of their comrades and they exchanged hugs, slaps on the back and handshakes.

George and all the men felt a great relief as the approaching column came into view, but his happiness was multiplied when he saw the colors of the relief column and instantly knew that their relieve was coming from the Buffalo Soldiers of the Tenth Cavalry.

Chapter 18

The Trip Home

It took several days for the men to recuperate from their ordeal and many of them left for their homes or back to their military assignments. The departing men knew that they had shared an unholy experience and felt lucky to be alive.

Steve was the one who had come out of the ordeal with a feeling of pleasure. The interpreters had brought news the Roman Nose had died a few hours after Steve had made his fantastic shot.

In a few weeks George learned that next month the company would be reassigned to Fort Gibson. He took this news with mixed emotion. He had always considered Gibson his home, but the move would also mean that from time to time he would be faced with Luge and that brought back many unpleasant feelings.

The next month passed rapidly and the movement of his company, despite the riggers, was about the most enjoyable time he had spent in the army. They arrived at Fort Gibson on a bright day and were sent to quarters east of the Parade grounds. They realized they were not to be quartered with the rest of the troops.

Ellen was overjoyed that they had returned and that she could resume some contact with her mother and father. George made the trip to the farm as seldom as he could. He saw no need to create conflict and distance seemed the best answer.

He paid more attention to his daughter and was delighted that Georgia had grown enough that she was now talking and responding to his presence. She was the greatest pleasure that he had experienced in some time. In no time she had him under her control. Her beautiful, big brown eyes and the dimples on her dark cream colored face seeming to cast a spell on him. She quickly learned that anytime she wanted attention she simply had to smile and hold out her arms. She had learned early how to control a man and used it to her advantage.

While the reestablishment of his family was rewarding for Ellen, the situation at the farm had changed little. Luge was still hell bent on exercising his authority and the housing situation had not changed. Ellen soon became tired of her husband's resistance to visits and told George to find them a place so she could live with him. She said if he could that she would be happy to go back to work in the laundry to help pay the expenses. In a short time George was able to secure a house across the river and move his family there. The relocation now gave George even more time with his family and he did not have to deal with a stubborn and unreasonable father-in-law.

Just as she had promised, Ellen became a civilian employee of the fort. The family's income was supplemented and the cost of the move was more than covered with her work as a seamstress and laundry helper.

Her new job was grueling and she soon experience conflict with a woman named Louise that seemed to think that she was the boss of the laundry. Louise continually criticized the work that Ellen did and seemed to have the same remarks for most of the women who worked with her.

Ellen soon had her fill of the bitch, "I don't see no strips on your fat sleeve and if you don't shut your mouth I is gonna shut it for you!"

"Really you ain't got the salt for what your mouth just said"

Louise then reached for a paddle that was used to stir the clothes in the boiling pots.

Before she had lifted it from the floor, Ellen hit her with a totally water soaked sheet that she had just started to wring out. The heft of the sheet with the force that Ellen exerted knocked the loud mouth to the floor.

Before, Louise could even start to gather herself from the shock of the attack and the water that covered her from head to toe, Ellen was standing over her with the paddle half drawn back, "You mouth off one more time to me or any of the ladies here and I'll shut your mouth for good. There ain't no one pushin' me around. I'll beat your ass till you can't stand up and then I'll cut your heart out!"

Louise held her hand up in front of her face and said, "No more." The next day Louise did not report to work and never returned.

Lieutenant Olsen stepped forward and addressed the men. Olson had arrived two days before and this was his first day to be assigned to a patrol.

He showed his dedication to his assignment with his spit and polished dress. He evidently had been taught at the military academy that you must be in control of your men at all times and that you had to demonstrate your authority by your appearance and vocal commands.

Truth was, he exhibited his lack of experience and his discomfort with his new assignment. This officer was so wet behind the ears that it was nearly laughable to the veterans of Company F. But as veterans and well disciplined troopers they held their stoic positions while the Lieutenant delivered his speech and exercised his authority.

Master Sergeant Goldsby could not help but glance down the line of his veteran troops with the hopes that he did not see one of his men break out into a laugh, while Olson continued his rant about the dangers and the responsibility that his patrol must shoulder on this assignment.

At last, Olson turned the men over to George and he immediately ordered the men to mount up and form a column of two. They were soon on the way into the territory and headed toward Muskogee.

It was one of those days that often come in the Territory. The wind was piercing cold and yet the heat from the sun let you know that spring was on its way. As the patrol made its way south toward the assigned railroad inspection a thunderous eruption of gun fire floated on the north wind. This was no hunting party someone was heavily involved in the exchange of gunfire.

The troopers put their mounts in full stride and headed in the direction of the hostility. Goldsby and Olson led the troopers toward the high ridge that was separating the advancing party from the continual roars of the obvious gun fight. They rapidly road up the ridge and slowed their mounts as they reached the crest.

Olson raised his hand and the troopers came to a halt, just before they reached the summit. He then ordered the men to dismount and George told two troopers to stay and hold the horses and the others rushed on foot to the top of the high ridge.

From their position they observed the valley and saw a man prone on the ground. He was thrashing in pain and kept lifting himself up and grasping his leg. The ground around him was littered with bed rolls and other evidence that this had been a night camp for several men. One unusual thing about the camp was that there were three large boxes scattered among the now abandoned bedrolls. The camp fire was still smoldering and a coffee pot could be seen still perched on a rock that had been used to encircle the campfire.

The observation was quickly diverted by the numerous clouds of gun smoke coming from the trees that were a few yards behind the campsite. The evidence of the length of the battle was that the valley now had a gray haze of gun smoke that filled the once clear and crisp morning air.

The crack of a Winchester came from a point to the left of the valley pinpointed the position of the men's attacker. The large black man was nestled in a perfect rock fortress and was delivering just enough fire to keep all of those hidden in the trees pinned to their positions.

After a few moments Olson said, "Sergeant, have your men fire on that man in the rocks."

Goldsby said, "Sir, I think that it would be better if me and Private Johnson just slipped down behind him and arrested him. We've no idea what's the cause of this conflict and it'd be better if we took 'im in and let the court decide what his fate should be."

Olson thought for a minute and then said, "I think you're right. Take Johnson and see it you can accomplish that. I'll have the others keep him in their sights in case he notices your advance and fires on you."

As soon as the two troopers became visible to the men in the trees on the other side of the valley they started to make moves back up the ridge to their rear some immediately grabbed their horses and tried to make their way up the ridge hidden by the cover of the trees. The others scampered by foot up the incline in hopes of reaching their now scattered horses.

Before Goldsby and Johnson could reach their destination the big, black man had turned and started back toward his horse that was tied in the trees behind him. He saw the advancing troopers and dropped his rifle to his side. "What in the hell are you doing here?" He bellowed at the approaching troopers. "You're lettin' those bastard whiskey runners get away!"

The two troopers froze in their tracks, with their carbines at the ready. "Who the hell are you?"

"I'm Bass Reeves, US Marshal and I have been trailing those sons-of-bitches for two days and now you're lettin' 'em get away!" He pulled his coat back and the star on his chest left now question as to who he was.

Goldsby said, "Sorry sir, we thought you were a bushwhacker tryin' to rob those men in the valley and you are lucky that we didn't fire on you from the ridge."

"Well, you'd a made a big mistake if you had, but let's get to our horses and ride those bastards down."

At that moment Goldsby looked up the ridge and found it abandoned. He was starting to reply when he saw Olson and the rest of the troopers clear a large out cropping of rocks and enter the valley at full speed. They entered the trees and were obviously in full pursuit of the fleeing men.

"Sir, I don't think you have to worry about the men escaping I promise my men 'll ride 'em down in good order."

"I sure hope you're right I don't like to come up empty handed and I've put in enough time that I should've had a passel of men in custody by now."

"Well sir, I am confident in my men and I know they'll bring back what they can. On top of that you already have one on the ground so you want be empty handed."

Bass thought for a moment and seemed to calm. He then said, "Well so this isn't a total loss let's go down and get some coffee. I was right careful not to hit the pot. I haven't had a thing all mornin' and had planned to get some warmin' from that pot all the time I was tryin' to capture those bastards."

His face now displayed a smile and both of the troopers nodded in approval.

While they were turning to start the descent, Goldsby said, "Private, go up the ridge and get our horses. We'll meet you at the campfire."

Bass took the reins of his big sorrel stallion and they worked their way down the craggy ridge.

As they approached the camp the man on the ground shouted, "You son-of-a-bitch you broke my leg!"

"Well, you should be happy that I didn't put one in your ear. You fire on a marshal and all you can expect is to pay a price."

Bass walked toward the coffee pot and took a tin from his saddle bag. By the time he had made sure the prone man was relieved of his pistol he was greeted by Goldsby and a hot pot of coffee. Goldsby poured him a cup and then raffled through the bedrolls until he came up with a cup for himself. The two placed both hands around the cup as they absorbed the warmth.

While they were refreshing themselves they heard intermittent gun fire in the far distance.

Goldsby smiled and said, "I told you my boys would run 'em bastards down. My men are some of the best and I knowed they would make your day better if we just gave 'em a chance."

He then dropped his head and looked at the smoking cup and after a few moments lifted his head and looked directly at Bass. "I've heard of you ever since I've been in the territory and have wanted to meet you, but I never thought I'd meet you by spoilin' your day."

"Well, if your men bring back the bastards it'll be OK. I can't get to bent out of shape, it want be the first time that people took me for the bad man. Seems to run with the fact that I am black and I'm sure you can understand that."

Goldsby shook his head, "Seems that most people think that the color of our skin is a sign that we is some kind of devil or somthin', but my men and I've pulled a bunch of folks asses out of some bad shit and maybe some of 'em will remember that without us they would've been in a heap of trouble."

"Well, we can hope, but it seems to me the more we do the less we're thought of, except for the ones we help at the moment."

Bass turned to the boy on the ground and handed him a cup of coffee. "I guess you be needin' this 'bout now. How old are you?"

He was still massaging his leg as he reached for the cup. "I'm sixteen."

"That's too young to be playin' a man's game and I figure that a few months in the calaboose will teach you a hard lesson. I truly hope it does, 'cause the next time we meet I don't want to have to put one where you want be gettin' over it."

While they were talking a few of the troopers started to return to the camp site. Each had a man under their control and one had a man slung over his horse.

Goldsby looked up as they returned and said, "I told you they were the best and I'm sure pleased that they proved me right."

"Looks like you were right and I hope that next time we meet it ain't quite as confusin'."

George looked at the returning men and slowly walked over to look at the horses there whiskey runners were on. He stroked his chin and then turned to Bass.

"Marshal, I see there're a couple of horses here, that look pretty fit and I was wonderin' if you'd mind us swappin' out a couple of my boy's horses for 'em? You see we is responsible for keepin' our own mounts and the way we do that is keepin' what we can from those we catch. That way we can keep or mounts in as good a condition as we can."

"I know you fellers has the same job I do and if it'll help you to relieve me of some of my problems you're welcome to 'em."

During the exchange Lieutenant Olson returned with the last of the bootleggers. He had a smile on his face, but still tried to act as though it was just a part of his job and he had done it many times.

George Goldsby introduced him to Bass and made a short but somewhat digging comment that he should be glad that they had not complied with his order to fire on the black man.

Handshakes and wishes for success were shared and Bass took his captives in tow, while the troopers returned to the trail for their inspection of the work crews that were laying track for the railroad.

Chapter 19

The Trouble

George had eaten his breakfast in the comfort of his rented house with Ellen and had spent over an hour playing and cuddling his daughter. He so enjoyed this week-end family times, but he had promised his friend, Joseph Tall Chief, that he would come and discuss with him some of the problems he and his Indian neighbors were facing from the encroachment of white men onto their grazing lands. It was only a few miles to the Tall Chief house and he had known Joseph for many years and just felt it was right to take his free time to see what the situation was. He hoped that with this first hand information he could convince Lieutenant Olson to put a special effort into the matter.

On the trip, he came across Private Washington setting beside the road under a shade tree holding his horse's reins in one hand and swigging on a bottle of whiskey with the other.

"What in the hell do you think you're doing Private? You know it's illegal to have whiskey in the territory. If I was you I'd be pourin' that on the ground immediately so I don't have to put you on report."

Washington swayed as he looked up at Goldsby and seemed to not be that concerned about the comments he had received. He finally struggled to his feet and still swaying said, "But Sergeant, it's our day off and I was needin' to relax."

"I don't give a shit what your reasons are, it is against the law, the law that we enforce and if you don't pour that out now you'll pay dearly for it."

Washington still swayed as he looked at the bottle and then little by little let the contents pour to the ground. "Now, does that make you happy?"

"Better, now get on your horse and get someplace and sober up." "How 'bout I rides along with you for a spell? There's a creek up the

way and I can take a dip there."

"Sounds okay with me, just get yourself together man. I'm goin' right by the creek. I'm headin' to my friends house and he lives there on the creek."

They parted company next to a large cluster of willow trees and George continued on a few hundred yards to Joseph's small secluded house.

Joseph greeted him warmly and while he had his arm around his neck escorted him into the small room and kitchen area of his humble home. Joseph's wife was there and she immediately poured coffee for the men and took her seat at a table and continued to work at the piece of leather that was spread before her.

Their conversation was friendly, as they discussed the many good times they had shared at the Beck house and there were even some laughter exchanged in these discussions. Finally, Joseph's expression changed and he started to tell George about all the problems he and his neighbors were having with white men grazing their cattle on Indian land. He went on to say that not only had the men resisted when they had been warned, but that there had been a time or two when they had pulled their pistols. There had even been one event where they had actually fired shots at the Indians, as they had approached them to complain again.

George excused himself and said that he had to return to his house, but promised to take the matter up with the officers at the Fort the next day.

He had only gone a short distance when he saw Washington's horse tied to a tree. He pulled up to the horse and dismounted figuring that

Washington had passed out and probably needed to be revived and assisted back to the fort.

To his surprise he found Washington leaning up against a tree near his horse and he was fully conscious. He had a slight grin on his face and seemed to be as happy as any trooper could be on a day off.

"Sergeant, I want to thank you for today." "How's that Private?"

"Well, you had me pour out my whiskey and instead I got here and had one hell of a real good time," he was still smiling and had picked a stem from the ground and was cleaning his teeth with it.

"Private, explain yourself."

"I had a hell of a good time poken that Injin girl till I couldn't hardly stand up."

George froze for a moment and attempted to assess the story being told him.

"What Indian girl are you talkin' about?"

"The one that was in the creek takin' a bath when I got here. She's still over there if you'd like to have a go at 'er. She want complain, I think she is still knocked out. He followed this statement with sinister laugh.

Goldsby now bristled and walked the few feet to the creek bank. The

Indian girl was motionless. There was blood running from the corner of her mouth and a very obvious knot on the side of her head. As George stooped down to see if he could assist the totally naked girl he realized that it was Joseph's little twelve year old daughter.

George was suddenly out of control, "God damn, what in the hell've you done you stupid black son-of-a-bitch?"

He then reached down and tried to see if she was alive. There was a slight pulse and he could see a slight heave of her naked breast, but only so slight and so infrequent.

George stood and looked down on this beautiful little girl that he had known since she was a baby. His thought turned to his own daughter and he knew that Joseph had the deep love for her as he had for his own.

George turned on his heels and quickly returned to where Washington was now standing and trying to mount his horse.

George grabbed Washington's shoulder and spun him around. He struck him as hard as he could with a right that caught Washington on the side of the head. The blow knocked him into the side of his horse, which bolted and ran out from under the force of the propelled body, causing Washington to hit the ground.

Washington had a reputation as a barroom fighter and this blow which would have put any ordinary man out cold only seemed to ignite his automatic response. "What the hell is wrong with you? She's only a Injin."

"Guess what you low life bastard she is my friends daughter and my daughter and my wife is only a Indian. I'm gonna kill you for what you've done."

Washington had gotten to his feet while this exchange had taken place and now a smile came to his face as blood trickled from the side of his mouth. "Goldsby, I've long wanted to kick the hell out of all the bastards givin' me orders and looks like today is the day."

He lowered his head and rushed George, but George stepped to one side and planted a solid right to the attacker's ribs. To his surprise the blow didn't even seem to faze him. As he stumbled for his footing he grabbed George and wrestled him to the ground.

They were both entangled in each other's arms and their legs were struggling to get traction as they each throw punches that had little power even if they had found there mark.

They struggled until they had both gained their footing and Washington threw a punch that caught George above the eye. Blood immediately started to run down his face and into his eye. George threw up his arm and blocked the following blow, but was caught in the right rib cage with the pursuing shot. He felt the air rush from his body and he sank to his knees. He then felt the weight of Washington completely overpower him as he was thrust back to the ground and felt the strong hands of his opponent grasp his throat. In seconds what little air he had left seem to lose it effects to keep him alive.

He desperately tried to force the hands from his throat, but found it totally useless. In desperation he franticly reached for his boot and grasps the handle of his knife. With one swift thrust he sank the blade to the hilt in Washington's left side.

He felt the relief come to his throat as air suddenly was allowed to enter. He gasped for more of this life giving substance, but at the same time withdrew his knife and sent it home again.

Now, Washington fell forward covering George's face with his body. George released the knife handle and pushed the now relaxed body

from his face. He struggled to his feet and wiped the blood from his eye that had now totally swollen shut. He looked down on Washington and was surprised to see him still smiling.

"Well, I think you killed me."

George silently stared down on the man and the indignation he felt from Washington's deeds still was not quenched.

"You'll only wish it was over in a minute."

"George grasped the long black locks of the immobile man and pulled his head up from the ground. He jerked his knife from the Private's side and instantly started to remove the victim's scalp. He pulled his knife slowly across Washington's forehead and at the same time pulled as hard as he could with his other hand, whose fingers were entwined in the black course hair. With each inch he pulled the razor sharp blade around Washington's head the harder he pulled on the hair in his hands.

Washington was bellowing like a castrated bull. He was trying to reach Georges hands, but had lost so much blood that the struggle was futile.

When the scalp finally broke free, George lifted it high in the air and suddenly he recalled all of the scalped men, women and children he had seen in Kansas.

Washington suddenly stopped his hollering. His hands fell to his side and his chest stopped moving up and down.

George slipped his leg out from under his head and he stood.

He stared at the scalp in his hands and suddenly flung it into the creek. George stood silent for a moment. He then pulled his pistol and fired it once and then a short time later the second time, across the creek.

George turned and rushed to Joseph's daughter's side. She was still breathing. He hurriedly removed his shirt and covered her nakedness as best he could. With some effort he lifted her and started running toward Joseph's house.

He did not have to run far, as Joseph was running toward him with his rifle in his hands. He screamed when he saw his daughter in George's arms and broke from a trot to an all out run.

When he reached George he grabbed his daughter and pulled her to his chest and started to rock her, as if she was a baby.

George grabbed him by the shoulders and turned him toward the house. He assisted Joseph with his trip to the front room and helped Joseph place her in the bed.

Joseph's wife immediately started administering as mush aid as she knew how and the two men stood in silence.

After the girl seemed to be breathing better Joseph asked, "What in the hell happened here?"

"I don't exactly know. When I got there, there were two Indians torturing a fellow soldier and I went to help. We had a long fight and I finally ran 'em off. I tried to shot 'em, but they scooted into the trees. I then found Ruth down by the creek and started to bring her back to the house.

"Bless you, my friend."

"Joseph, I have to go, but if you want I'll have a doctor come out as soon as I get to town."

"That want be necessary, I am goin' to hitch the team and take her in as soon as I can."

"I'll help you and then be headin' on."

The next day Lieutenant Olson asked Goldsby what had taken place. He had a doubtful look about him as he continued the questioning.

"So you say that you were returning from Joseph's home when you came upon two Indians beating Washington and you tried to stop them?

"Yes sir."

"Why didn't you pull your pistol?"

"Sir, I thought I could stop them and arrest them without any shootin'."

"I see. Then you had a fight with these men."

"Yes sir, I think that my condition is proof of that."

"Then you say you fired on them while they were trying to escape and missed both shots. I find that very surprising as well as you shot."

"Sir, they were runnin' through the trees and I's pretty badly beaten, again as you can see. They did drop somethin' in the creek when I fired the second shot."

"Let me ask you one more time. Did you like Washington and had you ever had a run in with him in the past?"

"Sir, I knew Private Washington as a trooper. I had only had him in my unit one time and I had never had a run in with 'im or written 'im up on any occasion."

"Well, that will be all. I am going to check your story and if it proves to be as you say I will be the first to congratulate you for your deeds with the little girl and your actions to save Washington. You are dismissed."

As George turned to go to the door, Olson said, "We have been ordered to move to Camp Wichita in the western part of the Territory and I will be taking you and an advanced Company out next week to make preparations for the others.

"Yes sir, will my wife and daughter be allowed to come along?"

"Not at this time. I know she's doing laundry here at the fort and she will be able to continue that in your absence. When we get settled in at the camp your family will be transported to the new location and she will continue her duties there."

Chapter 20

Camp Wichita

This might have been supposedly a camp, but what Goldsby and his men found was only a great and beautiful area nestled in the mountains and surrounded by great grazing land and an abundance of wild life.

General Grierson soon had all the men hard at work constructing housing and buildings for the coming troops. The work was hard and the demands were great, but the skill level of the troopers increased daily and in a short time the grounds started to look like a formidable outpost.

By the time Ellen and Georgia arrived most of the 10th were in place and rather than a fighting unit they had turned into skilled laborers. The labor was broken everyday by military drills, which seemed at the time a waste, as there were no encounters with hostiles and it looked as though there wouldn't be. However, the General had his reasons and the officers demanded that the troopers preformed at their best.

George was walking across the parade grounds at about noon. He was headed toward the mess when a small contingent of solders entered the fort. He had to look twice in order to make sure of what he saw.

At the front of the troopers was a man who at first George thought had the most severe suntan he had ever seen. After taking a second look, he realized that the lieutenant leading the column was a Negro.

George had to simply stand and watch the man lead his troops to the headquarters building and dismount. He then turned and dismissed the men, wheeled in his shining boots and entered the building.

As soon as he disappeared into the building, George rushed to intercept the men as they rode toward the stables.

"Who the hell is that?"

The trooper had a smile on his face as he said, "That is Lieutenant Flipper, he's a West Point graduate and one hell of a feller. It is kinda nice to have a officer like him around us and I think he'll be a nice addition for this here fort."

"Well, I'll be damned, I'd a never thought it."

As time passed, it became obvious that the discipline of the Academy had made its mark on the man. He was as strict as any of the officers and seemed to demand more of the troopers than most.

Flipper's enthusiasm was evident when he ordered the troopers to dig a ditch near the swamp land that was near the fort. The men spent days in the hot sun and ankle deep in mud to accomplish the chore. Some of the men complained about the mud, but others felt that it was better than mining the limestone. It was finally concluded that it didn't matter that much, work was work.

It was during this time and while they were away from the white officers that he started to demonstrate that he was in need of a friend. He motioned for George to come out of the ditch and had him walk with him farther from the men.

"Sergeant, I am proud of you and your men. They are good and dedicated workers."

"Thank you sir, I think you'll find 'em as good in the field as they are as workers here."

"Sergeant, can I talk freely with you and what I say is between you and me?"

"Yes sir."

"It seems that, with the exception of a few, that most of the officers have a real problem with me being and officer I feel that are going to try to set me up in some way and I would like for you to keep an eye and ear out for any plan you might overhear. I have learned that most of the officers respect you and your work and if there is anyone who might get wind of something it would be you."

"Sir, you can count on me to be as watchful as if I was scoutin' for Indians and I surely will report it to you. I've a great respect for anyone who has come as far as you has and I sure don't want to let anythin' happen to you."

"Thank you, and please don't let the others know of my suspicions."

When the camp became an appropriate and recognizable fort, the General called a complete assemblage and proudly announced to the men his pleasure at their work and named this location Fort Sill.

The troopers were finally put into the field and their daily routine consisted of patrolling different areas of the massive lands that surrounded the fort. These patrols often encountered bands of marauding

Indians, but just as frequently white men who were horse thieves, gun runners and whiskey peddlers.

Most of the Indians were in small bands and their greatest skill was evading contact with the patrols. In a few instances small skirmishes took place, but in general there were few casualties on either side.

"Sergeant, come here let's talk about your men's actions today." "Yes sir, Lieutenant Pepoon."

"I just wanted to commend you and your troopers for a job well done. You preformed excellent tactics by surrounding those horse thieves and bringing them in and I am sure the owners of the horses you recovered will be very appreciative."

"Thank you, sir."

"I also want you to know that the attitude of your men is talked about among the other officers. They say that they have never been around a group that seems to never complain and your music and singing makes life here a little less uncomfortable."

"Well sir, General Grierson has a lot to do with that. You know we've been under his command off and on for many years now and he has taught us how to play some instruments and his old love of teaching music has made us feel more at home. You know for a music man he really is a hell of a fightin' man."

"I know, and a good commander"

"Sir, while we is talkin' I'd like to know a little 'bout you."

"Well, I served a lot of time in Oregon during the big war and I had my share and a few others share of fightin' Indians up there."

"I see sir, I had heard some of the officers call you the 'Indian huntin' cuss' and was a wonderin' how that happened."

"Well, I'm not real proud of that name, but some others hung it on me while I was up north and it just stuck."

"I see sir, I feel that we'll soon get a chance to add some stories to your list, all these here tribes seem to not be takin' kindly to all these white folks tryin' to move into their territory and I can kinda understand why."

"Well, I do too, but we have are orders to bring them up to the reservations no matter how they feel and as soldiers we have to follow orders. I know that you and the others in the 10th really respect the General, so I thought you should let you know that he is being replaced by a General Davidson next week. I ask you to kind of help get the men prepared for the change and I hope you will help make that transition as smooth as possible."

"Sir, I really hate to hear that, but we is soldiers and we do what needs to be done and will do it for whoever is in charge, and as long as they leave men like you here all should go well."

"I'll stay as long as they let me and again, I hope you pass the word that I am proud to be serving with you and your men."

"George I got a problem." "Ellen, what's eatin' at you."

"I hear things at work that makes me pretty upset and nervous at the same time."

"I hear that the Generals daughter is beddin' some of the officers and on top of that I hear one of the Lieutenant's wives is beddin' not only some of the other officers, but is beddin' some of the troopers of the 10th."

George cleared his throat and looked at the floor. He then walked to the other side of the room and with his hand behind his back turned and said, "Ellen, I've heard the same, but it's not my business and time usually makes things like his come to a head. It's not my duty to get involved in these matters and I hope it doesn't bother my men and their duty."

"Okay, I understand that, but the big question is, are you one of the men beddin' the Lieutenant's wife?

"George's eyes now looked directly at Ellen, as he cleared his throat and then replied, "The answer is no. I'm not even positive that it is really happenin'. You know how rumors get started on these here places and it seems the longer they go the bigger the story gets. I just want you to go back to work and keep that in mind. Don't let these things get under your skin. If they is happenin' it'll come out at a proper time."

"George you sure do spend a lot of time in the stable."

George's eyes narrowed as he stood up as straight as he would at full attention. "God damn it." He let a back hand go that caught Ellen full in the face and she staggered across the floor and feel into a chair.

"If you haven't, for some stupid reason, noticed that's where the horses are and the nags that has been issued us need all the care we can give 'em. It's my job to see that they are cared for as best we can."

Ellen pulled herself to an upright position and despite the tears running down her cheek said, "I'm told that the General's daughter has a cot out there in the stable and that's where all the messin' takes place and you tell me you know nothin' 'bout it."

"Lady, I do my job and that's it. I'm not responsible for anythin' the officers do and I ain't keepin' up with 'em. Now, I've had all of this talk that

I want and I'm tellin' you not to pay no never mind to what you hear. You can't believe a word of it and you can only believe about half of what you see. So drop this right now!"

George placed his hat on his head and headed out the door. "I've work to do and you askin' lots of questions ain't helpin' none."

George had only gone a few yards when he stopped. He slowly turned around and walked back to the shack. He politely knocked on the door and then with his hat in his hand entered.

He held his hat on his chest covering his heart and said, "Ellen, I love you and I love what we've done together. I know it ain't much, but it is sure better than most folks got. I'm sorry for a hittin' you, so sorry, but I have a idea and I hope you like it."

Ellen stood up from the chair and wiped her face and said, "What kinda idea you got?"

George cleared his throat. "You know all these years we has convinced people we was married."

He looked at the floor and then looked directly into her eyes.

"You know that church me and the men built with our own money and time, I was wonderin' if you'd like for me and you to go to the Chaplin tomorrow and have 'im make it official?"

"Ellen's face turned from a look of disgust and bewilderment into a smile. She rocked back on her heels, there was hesitation in her movement and then rushed toward George. She threw her arms around his neck and jumped upward wrapping her legs around his body. She then placed a long and deep kiss on his lips and slowly sighed, "Yes, tomorrow."

It was a blistering hot June day as the 10th assembled in the parade grounds of Fort Sill. The men had been prepared for this trip and were most anxious to get on the trail to what they hoped would be the last great conflict with the Indians.

General Davidson lead the full complement of men on the trail due west. They traveled at a brisk pace for they knew they had hundreds of miles to cover in order to get to the assigned position.

The further they traveled the less inhabitable the land became. In a short time trees started to disappear and creeks and streams became less frequent.

George thought to himself what a terrible country. Why would the

Indians so desperately protect this land and fight and die to stay here? Then he recalled what the need of freedom was like and started to realize how important that was. He remembered the past when he would have given his life just to have had the freedom to be able to do what he wanted when he wanted and the entire actions started to make sense to him.

After several days the 9th Cavalry broke from the ranks and headed in a more southwesterly direction. The 10th continued more northerly into the land that challenged the men in so many ways. The heat was nearly unbearable and the wind blew constantly. The wind should have been welcome, but it seemed to only intensify the discomfort.

Lieutenant Pepoon led George and his company on several scouting parties into the desolate land, while other officers did the same. They truly wanted to make contact with the hostiles, but continually came up empty handed.

The Lieutenant became very friendly with the company and joined the men in the evening after they had eaten. He seemed to delight in the music and good humor that seemed to always permeate the group.

One night, when all seemed to be relaxed the men started to talk of their past experiences and the subject of how the Indians in Kansas had been so brutal in their efforts to discourage the intrusion of settles to their area.

Pepoon finally joined the conversation and said, "Well, I know any mutilation of men and women and especially children has to have made an impression on all of you, but when I was in the Oregon territory I came upon a sight that I will never get out of my mind. I was scouting an area where we knew there was a lot of Indian activity and as we got closer to a mining camp we could see what seemed to be dozens of buzzards circling the area.

We know that this was a sign that we were about to be faced with something unpleasant, but were not prepared for what we found.

"As we entered the area there were just as many buzzards on the ground as we had witnessed in the air and they were flapping their wings and hopping from one dead Chinaman to the other. There was a total of fifty Chinamen spread out in all directions from their camp. They had all been scalped and most of them had had their nuts cut off. It was learned later that the Indians really took great pride in the Chinamen's scalp due to the long braids that they all possessed. I'm tellin' you that this sight along with the fact that the buzzards had picked the eyes out of most of the faces will long live in my mind."

George said, "Well, that is the worst I've heard and I was at Pickets charge. As bad as it was, there is something more tolerable about men gettin' killed in combat than mutilated by other men just for the hell of it."

The next morning brought a great surprise. A runner from the ninth came in and told that the Indians had been caught by the main contingent in a canyon and had nearly been wiped out. The army had captured nearly all of their horses and had burned all the housing along with capturing most of their food supply. The orders were for the 10th to pickup any and all stragglers and take them back to their reservation lands.

The scouting parties continued and one day about noon they spotted smoke coming from a valley. They divided their forces with Lieutenant Pepoon taking some men descending the creek bank about a mile north of the smoke and Sergeant Goldsby taking the other half far to the south of the smoke, where they entered the creek bed

Both bodies of men dismounted their horses and led them toward the intended target. They had expected the surprise to foil any resistance. However, this was not the case.

Sergeant Brooks stood when all the troops were in position and walked into the clearing. He held up his hand and in Cheyenne said, "Lay down your weapons and come peacefully with us."

To everyone's surprise the women grabbed their children and throw themselves on the ground and the twenty men took positions behind the meager bundles of supplies they were carrying. They immediately throw their rifles over their cover and fired at the Sergeant.

He threw himself flat on the ground and the Indians fire was met by a barrage of carbine discharges from both the north and south end of the creek bed.

The Indians evidently had no desire to surrender and had decided to fight to the end for their freedom. In less than a minute the creek bottom was filled with a thick cover of gun smoke and the smell of spent powder filled the thick air.

The exchange continued for several minutes and then the firing from the Indian encampment stopped. In one mad rush two of the warriors jumped their hastily made fortress They released bone chilling war cries, and with war clubs waving in the air ran directly at their attackers. They were met by a volley that dropped them in mid-stride.

The rest of the huddled group threw their rifles over the sides of their protection and in a few moments one shouted, "We surrender white eyes!"

The shaken, but safe, Brooks shouted for them to stand and show their hands, and they complied.

With all the troopers surrounding the haggled, group, Lieutenant Pepoon handed the women food from the trooper's saddle bags. He then did the same with the men. After their closely observed meal was finished,

Sergeant Brooks told them they would be escorted back to camp and held there, then be transferred to the Indian Reservation in Indian Territory.

The brief battle in the creek was the most hostility that the 10th encountered during their tour in the west The rest of their duties were picking up straggling groups of five to twenty Indians as they journeyed north hoping to somehow escape the horrors of what they had faced in the canyon earlier.

There was no more resistance. The Indians were defeated and most of them knew it. In fact, the conditions were so bad that most seemed to welcome being taken in where they could be feed and housed. Their days were over and while they still longingly stared around them at their land, as if they could stay forever in their minds, the taste of defeat and the end of their life as they had known it was now a thing of the past.

Chapter 21

The Undoing

The Indians were taken back to Fort Sill and in a very short time were dispersed to their assigned lands. The duties at the fort continued and it became obvious that while it should have been a time of great relief to the officers and the troopers the air was filled with hostility.

George could see that some officers were avoiding others and on a few occasions physical fights actually broke out between the officers. He also observed that some of the troopers seemed to be consistently selected for duties such as cleaning the latrines and mucking the stables.

These actions made his job much more difficult. Earlier there had been very little grumbling and discontent displayed among the troopers, now it seemed that each and every one of the men had something to complain about. The usual singing and music at night had stopped and the total fort seemed to be in a state of unrest.

Ellen even complained that the women in the laundry were now squabbling and having arguments, sometimes leading to hair pulling and kicking fights. Many times troopers were called in to separate the women and some were sent home.

Ellen said, "George it seems like this place is a huge kittle of water settin' over a roarin' fire and the water is starting to bubble and boil. I think a huge explosion is about to take place and it can all be blamed on all the drinkin', gamblin' and beddin' that has been goin' on."

"Well, I am havin' more problems with the troopers than I have ever had in all my years. I fear that there is gonna be some serious bloodshed here in the fort, maybe more than was shed in the Indian wars. Davidson seems to be upset all the time and the officers don't seem to give a good damn about anythin'."

It was a clear fall day and George had just finished assigning men to their duties when Lieutenant Pepoon motioned for him to come over by the little church. He pointed to a small bench and told George to set.

"Sergeant, you know I told you that the officers that disliked the way I treat the colored troops were planning on setting me up."

"Yes sir."

"Well, they have done it. Several of them have filed a complaint that I have been cheating at cards. The truth is I had one hell of a lucky streak and cleaned the table out. I didn't cheat and I swear to you everything that happened that night was just damned dumb luck. But they have insisted on filing the complaint, even when I told them I would return their losses. If they do this I am finished. It is a court marshal offence and I'll be busted out of the service. George this is all I know and what I love. It will be the end of me. I have spent nearly twenty years of my life serving my country the best I know how and I just can't think of any other life.

I have sent a telegraph to General Sheridan and ask for his help, but I have had no reply. I also sent a letter to his headquarters telling him of all the depravity that is taking place here. It is not like me to complain, but somethin' has got to be done. This fort should be a shining star for its accomplishments and instead it is a shit hole."

George pushed his hat back on his head and then placed his elbows on his knees as he slumped over on the bench. He looked up into Pepoon/s down turned eyes and said, "Sir, I know you're a good man and really good officer and I can't even think of you not bein' here. Surely they want bust you out after all you've done here and during the big war."

"The problem is I know it is going to happen and I just can't handle it. I only wanted to tell you what is taking place because I respect you and the work you do. I have a real likin' for you and someone I can trust needs to know what is going on. In my letter I named names. I am sure you know that General Davidson's daughter is getting poked by nearly everyman that cares to have a go at her, and I am sure you know that Lieutenant Myers' wife has done the same with most of the other officers including several of the married ones. I also know and reported that Davidson himself has sold whiskey to the officers and that he is getting kickbacks from the sutler and allowing them to raise their prices which is eating into every mans pocket. This I have done in hopes that my leaving will have some positive effect on the future here."

"Lieutenant, I hope you're wrong about getting' busted out and I sure do thank you for the kind words you have said about me and my men. I hope your letter does some good and no matter what happens it has been an honor to have served with you."

Pepoon stood and extended his hand and they shook with a great deal of feeling. He then stepped back and delivered a sincere and long salute to George who returned the same.

The next afternoon a trooper came into the fort at a full gallop. He hastily dismounted in front of the headquarters building and rushed inside. In less than ten minutes all in the fort knew that Lieutenant Pepoon had killed himself in a tent about eight miles from the fort.

It was a sad day for the men of the 10th. He had been one officer who had always shown respect to the colored troopers and treated them like men. His death seemed to have brought a feeling of calm to the troopers. The bickering and complaining suddenly stopped and the men realized that their past discontent was of no importance compared to the loss of their friend.

In less than a week an official inspection team arrived and in less than a week orders were given that the 10th would be immediately moved to Fort Concho close to the Mexican border.

Chapter 23

Fort Concho

Ellen said, "Well, if this is supposed to be an improvement I'd like to know how? The heat here makes the territory fell like spring and this place needs as much construction as Fort Sill did. I hope that the doctor here is better than the one at Sill, 'cause I think I will be havin' my baby any day now."

"The real good thing is that you didn't have it on the trail. It would've been a pretty nervous time for me. I just hope you have a boy this time. I love Georgia with all my heart, but I sure would like to have a son to make me proud. Of course, I will take whatever you bring me." George put his arm around her and squeezed her close to his body.

"I don't care how bad this place is it can't be any worse than where we came from and at least here we have General Grierson as the commanding officer and he's one hell of a man and I'm sure that he want let things get out of control like they was at Sill. I'd come nearer puttin' my life in his hands than any officer I've ever had."

Ellen was correct. In a few days she started to have labor pains and George took her to the Fort hospital.

Doctor Notson was a congenial man and he treated Ellen like she was his first patient. In fact, she was his first Negro patient, but he seemed to not have any hesitation in treating her and her new baby.

The doctor came out of the operating room and smiled as he told George the news that he was now the father of a baby boy.

George jumped to his feet and a huge smile covered his weather beaten face. He immediately grabbed Notson's hand and started pumping it like he was trying to get water from a dry well.

Notson pointed to a bench and ushered George to it. It was not clear if he did this as a friendly jester or as a means to get George to let go of his hand. The doctor took a seat next to him and placed his arm around his shoulder.

"What are you going to name the little fellow?

"I'm gonna call him Crawford for my brother that I've not seen since we were separated when we were slaves. I have no idea where he might be. We was pretty close and they just up and separated us."

The doc shook his head and said, "It is hard for me to even think about me being separated from my brother and I can sure understand why you would want to do that.

"I know you and your men are new here and I just want to warn you and ask you to warn your men about the town across the river. If you want a taste of hell all you have to do is cross the Concho. There is more killing and fights there in one day than most of you have seen in your years of service. The town is made up of nothing but whore houses and bars and the most common residents are the buffalo hunters, this tied to the gamblers and whores makes for a deadly combination. I am telling you that in the last year there have been more than one hundred murders and that is in a town that usually doesn't have more than three hundred people living there.

"What I am telling you is that all of you should stay away and if you don't I can only wish you well and hope the good lord is looking after you.

"Now I know that most of you colored men don't mind fighting, that is why you are in the cavalry, but there isn't anything fair about the way they fight. The fact that you fellows are black sure isn't going to set well with most of the inhabitants. Most are ex-confederate soldiers and if they weren't they sure have the blood of the south running in their veins.

"It is beyond me why they send you colored fellows here in the first place.

All I can think of is they wanted to rub the people's nose in it for the war and that isn't going to be healthy for anyone involved."

"I think you sir for your warnin' and I sure'll pass it on, but you need to know my boys are as tough as any and they ain't to be trifled with. If the stupid confederates want to get down and dirty I fear they will come out with mud all over 'em. But I'll pass it on anyway and we'll just have to wait and see what happens."

The duties at Concho were not much different from Fort Sill. The men escorted mail coaches, built roads, continued construction on the fort, chased Indians after they had struck settlers or processions of settlers trying to establish new homes. The new challenge they faced was the Mexican bandits that crossed the border and then fled back to the safety of their own country.

Those that were not doing work on the fort were continually on patrol. These patrols were in search of any civil disturbance occurring in the territory, but often ended up being notations of passes, water sources, and grazing lands.

The allure of San Angelo was just too great for all of those stationed at the fort. They were men and hard working men and had need of diversions.

The saloons and whore houses on the other side of the river were designed to meet those needs.

Despite all the warnings from George, the lieutenants and General Grierson the temptations were just too great.

The town had received the enlisted and officers from the fort for some time, and developed a history of harsh treatment, but had never been exposed to men of color who not only were strangers, but had authority. The town was brimming with southern pride, in spite of them being on the losing side of a war, the citizens did not believe they had really lost.

The first few trips into town were met with hostile looks and many vile and contemptuous words. The men only found one saloon that would serve them and just a few ladies of the night that saw money more important than southern pride.

Slowly the smell of fresh money changed service to the men, but the hostile attitudes of the residents never slackened. In fact, the men started reporting that on several occasions shots were fired at them from darkened alcoves in the buildings. These shots were surely not meant to kill for at the distance any shooter definitely could have hit their mark. It was just taken as an elevation in the harassment.

The lure of the offerings of the town just was too enticing and while a few decided that the dangers were too great, most continued spending their free time and hard earned money where they felt they could get the most enjoyment.

The men knew never to go alone and usually traveled in at least groups of six or more. These numbers seemed to provide some deterrent to the challenges often given by people on the streets or present in the saloons.

After many close calls the day finally came when all the simmering hatred came to a boil. While a group of the men had gone on their usual adventurous trip. Two had decided to stay, evidently fortified by too much whiskey, while the others returned to the fort. Their bravery or foolishness soon led to the long expected conflict.

The Sergeant turned to the two privates as they lifted another shot glass to their lips and said, "Let's go boys it's time to hit the bunks."

Corporal Thompson turned to him as he replaced his empty glass to the bar and said, "I'm stayin' till Walters gets through with his lady and then we'll be right there."

"Corporal I said that it was time to go."

"I know what you said and you heard me."

"Corporal, do I have to give you an order?"

"We ain't on the grounds and I is on my free time and I'll spend it like I want."

The sergeant looked around the dingy and smelly barroom. There were several men setting at a table, obviously buffalo hunters by their dress and mannerisms. These men kept drinking, but surely were paying attention to what was taking place at the bar. There were four others setting at the table playing cards, in the corner. They were regular customers and had never dis-played open hostility to any group that the Sergeant had been with previously.

However, the defiant attitude of the corporal could not go unnoticed.

While he was assessing the crowd Private Walters entered the front door with a smile on his face. He immediately walked to the bar and ordered a shot.

"Private, we were just leaving and want you and the corporal to come along."

"Come on Sergeant. I need a drink to replenish my bodily fluids," he said with a smile on his face."

The bar keeper had placed his glass in front of him and he slowly tipped the glass to his lips.

"Okay, boys I've ask you and now I see that you have made up your minds to stay so you are no longer my responsibility. Get back to the fort as soon as you can."

He and the others turned and left.

It was nearly two in the morning when a knock came on George's door. The knock was quickly followed by someone shouting, "Sergeant, come quick we got a problem."

George hastily left the bed and put his trousers on and pulled his gallowses up over his shoulders. When he opened the door the lantern light caused him to blink and slightly turn away. "What's the problem?"

"Two of our boys had a hell of a fight in town and hardly made it back to the fort. They is bunged up pretty bad and the bastards has insulted all of us by rippin' their strips and chevrons off of their uniforms. We has had enough of the humiliation the no good ass holes is handin' out and want to do somethin' 'bout it."

"Well, go back and kick the hell out of 'em"

"We aim to, but they is totin' guns and we ain't got none. We want you to is-sue us our arms to make it even we'll do the house cleanin' that needs to be done."

George stood for a moment. He glanced from the lantern light into the darkness. His silence was broken by, "You know those confederate bastards has harassed us about as long as we can take it.

"Let me get my boots on and my keys and I'll be there in a minute."

In the door to the armory George, after dispensing the arms said, "Now, boys you know this is just to make it even. Don't go to shootin' up the place; just beat the Holy hell out of that bunch of bastards."

"That's what we is a plannin' on. A good ass whippin' might change a lot of people's minds 'bout messin' with us."

As the men left the fort George turned and went to the bunk house.

The room was lit with the lanterns and he had no trouble finding Walters and Thompson.

There was a crowd of troopers, standing around them as they set on their bunks. Each man had a blood soaked towel and was attempting to stop the bleeding from the wounds on their heads.

The six men hesitated as they approached the dimly lit Saloon and looked at each other. Brown said, "I is tired of this shit and we is the one's that can put an end to it. They then smiled and all nodded, as they proudly walked through the door and went directly to the bar.

"Give us a bottle of whiskey!"

Jim, the bar keep stood for a moment. The men's entrance had taken him back and the appearance of so many with such a look of purpose was a total surprise.

Jim nervously placed a bottle on the bar and slowly placed six glasses in front of the men. All of these motions were automatic, but his focus was on the table of buffalo hunters who had previously been sharing laughter and slaps on the back.

The men poured their drinks and quickly slapped them down. In one move they slammed their glasses to the bar.

They wheeled as if it had been a command and faced the two tables of hunters and cowboys on the other side of the room.

There was a tension filled silence that seemed to have no ending, until Brown said, "We is here to kick your ass. You have trifled with us once to many times and we has took it, but you have disgraced our uniform and by doin' that you have disgraced our country and what we stand for."

One of the hunters shouted, "You bunch of stinkin' niggers couldn't kick any ones ass." He then threw the strips and chevrons at the group and said, "Start your kickin."

The first step toward the men brought pistols from the sides of the hunters and cowboys and as they were reaching the top of the tables an equal move was being made by the standing, troopers.

The first shots from the hunters seemed to all be directed toward Private

Brown. He slumped forward and then took a nose dive to the floor. The trained troopers had already picked their marks and when they pulled the triggers of their colts six of the men behind the table fell in different directions. All the explosions from the pistols sent a deafening rumble through the room and were mixed with the sound of falling tables and shattering glass. For every shot fired by an opponent the troopers delivered at least two in response.

The room was instantly filled with gun smoke and the smell of the powder quickly overcame the rancid odder that had previously incased the room.

One of the downed cowboys got off a shot as he was falling, but it was wide of the mark and only added another tinkling of glass as it dislodged the remaining fragment of mirror that had once served as the backdrop to the bottles that had stood on the shelf behind the bar.

The troopers hurriedly grabbed Brown and hoisted him to their shoulders. There training in rhythmic movement took over and they smoothly exited the now obliterated interior of the building.

This day at the fort was truly a memorable one. It certainly was not the same hum-drum boring setting. Officers were rushing from building to building and the troopers were gathering in groups listening to the latest scuttlebutt as it was being transferred from unit to unit. These clusters were often broken up by cheers and the slapping of backs.

Those men who had been identified when they had returned to camp were soon standing at attention in front of the headquarter building, with a Lieutenant standing on each side of them.

One by one they were called and disappeared into General Grierson's. By mid-day a Lieutenant had found Goldsby at the stables. He had escorted him back to Grierson's office and had opened the door and motioned the Sergeant in.

Grierson sat at his desk. The fact that he was unshaven and his clothes somewhat disheveled showed that his day had not stated in its usual fashion. He lifted his head as Goldsby entered and looked at the Sergeant from head to foot. He then rose and started around his desk toward where Goldsby was standing at attention.

"Sergeant, I have been informed that you were the one who furnished the troopers with firearms. Is that true?"

With his eyes straight ahead, Goldsby replied, "Yes sir."

"Do you know that those actions cost the life of one of your troopers? "Yes sir."

"Do you know that the issuing of weapons is forbidden?" "Yes sir."

"Do you know that at least two citizens were killed by the use of these weapons?"

"I've been told that sir."

"Do you know that I am going to have to fill out piles of paper work to explain the action of those men?"

"Yes sir."

"Do you know that I don't give a damn, because I feel the men were justified and that they were acting in response to an unprovoked attack on some of their own and more importantly unacceptable disrespect of the United States by a bunch of low life confederate sympathizes who had continually shown disrespect to the very people who are trying to make this area safe for God fearing, hard working people.

"While I am going to have to penalize you by making you forfeit 10 days pay, I am also proud of what you and the men did. If the idiot murders that live here and think that they are humans, just because they walk upright can't get over it then they can kiss my Yankee ass."

The General then stood directly in front of Goldsby and snapped, "You are dismissed." He then briskly returned the Sergeants salute.

Two days later a contingent of riders approached the main gate. The man at the head of the party, demanded to see the General.

When General Grierson finally appeared at the gate and the man said, "I am Captain Arrington of the Texas Rangers and I am ordering you to turn over a Sergeant Goldsby and all the others involved in the murder and woundin' of the fine Texas citizens night before last."

Grierson looked up at the man and said, "I am the commanding officer of this fort and have been given power to oversee any and all situations that may cause unrest in this area by the United States Department of War. You are now standing on Federal property and if you don't remove your fat ass I will have you and all with you arrested and tried for treason."

"Hell, you can't do that."

"Captain, if you doubt that, just set there for one more minute and see how quickly fifty carbines will be pointed straight at you."

Arrington's face wrinkled up like he had just bitten into a dill pickle and then he looked over his shoulder at the followers, who had already started turning their horses back across the river. He followed in quick time.

As Grierson turned and reentered the fort there was a moments of silence that was soon broken by cheers from the men.

That afternoon Grierson met the men in the parade ground as they were preparing for another patrol.

"I want all of you to know that I am deeply saddened by the loss of Private Brown, but I also want you to know that I think he died in an act of bravery in defense of the United States of America.

"I do not want this to happen to another trooper under my command, so I ask you to continue your patrols and assignments with vigor and honor. Please be extra vigilant and be more cautious than usual when you approach people that you think should be friendly. In fact, approach all you meet as if they are the enemy."

In about three months a Texas Ranger came to the front gate and deliv-ered a Court order that demanded that George and the others report to the Texas Court on charges of Murder, assault with intent to kill, aiding in illegal acts and so many other charges that it took a full page to list them all.

Grierson called the men in and explained that he had done all he could. That as long as they were on Federal property he felt that he could keep them from being arrested, but since Texas was a state and not like Indian Territory, there was little he could do.

George went to the house early that evening and tried to figure out how the Rangers knew that he was the one who supplied the arms for the shoot-out. He was positive that none of the men involved would have told.

To ease his mind he tried to distract himself by playing with Georgia, she was now seven and had become a bundle of activity and seemed to love any attention she could get from her father.

The thing that George loved about her most was that she had become such a caretaker for little Crawford. She cuddled him and tried to assist him in anything that a two year old might want to do are explore. It seemed that Craw-ford was becoming more spoiled than she had ever been. If he wanted some-thing he wanted it now and if he felt like he wasn't getting enough attention he quickly found some way to get it. This usually was accomplished by throwing a fit or screaming at the top of his voice, until he got what he wanted.

George and Ellen felt that they had been blessed to find Aunte Amanda Foster as a house keeper and a babysitter. They did not have much money, but she was black and her husband had died and she had no place to live, so providing her with a place to live and feeding her was a far better deal than she could have received from anyone if San Angelo. She had become a part of the family and both of the children were exposed to her presence as much as their mother's, because Ellen had continued to work, which supplied some extra money and an extra food ration from the Fort.

When Ellen got home she noticed that George was withdrawn.

"What is on your mind?"

"Ellen, I just can't figure how the Rangers found out that I was the one who let the men in the armory that night?"

"Is that all you need"

"Hell, that's a plenty"

"Yea, but it is simple"

"How is that?"

"You know us ladies in the laundry ain't just workers. We spend a lot of time not just cleaning the shit out of drawers, but while we is doin' that we talk about all the dirt around the Fort.

"You know that Corporal Robertson has a girlfriend in San Angelo. At least he thinks he is in love with a whore they call Linda, but all she is doin' is takin' him for his money and playin' like she loves 'im.

"Well, the Rangers knew that and they got her to work the poor bastard into tellin' all the names of those involved and who furnished them with the guns."

"You mean my Corporal?"

"The one and only."

"How in the hell did you find this out?"

"One of the ladies in the laundry is a friend of this Linda girl. In fact, I think she works in the same house when she ain't workin' here. She got a cou-ple of kids and no man, so she gotta be doin' somehin' to make ends meet.

"Anyway one day she was a talkin' 'bout all that was involved in the ruckus and slowly but surely let it slip that she knew their names 'cause Linda had told her and that Linda was a plannin' on leavin' town 'cause the Rangers had set her up in a better place in Austin that catered to politicians."

"Well, I'll be damned. I had figured that maybe the barkeep or one of the survivors had known the men by name, but just couldn't figure how they had got mine. And this explains it."

George turned and went to the table. He pulled back a chair and when he sat he leaned forward and put his head in his hands.

Ellen approached his back and started to rub his neck. "You sure is tense. What else is eatin' you?"

"Would a little good news help yea?"

"I can't imagine any good news at this here time." "Well, how about that I'm gonna have another baby?"

"Damn, any other time that would be great, but we got too many problems for that to do anything but trouble me more.

"Ellen don't you realize that if that bunch of Confederate gets their hands on me or any of the boys that they is gonna hang use and do it with the blessin' of a court of Texas law?

"Ellen, I gotta get the hell out of here. I got a little money and I'll stay until the end of the month so you can get my pay. You and the kids and Aunte can stay here for at least another month, 'cause they can't move you until it becomes official that I'm AWOL.

"I'll head someplace and get you some money somehow. When you have to leave here you head back to your pa's place and I'll find you there, but I can only come in the nights 'cause the people at Fort Gibson knows where you'll probably be and knows that I'll show up some day and they'll be wantin' to arrest me for goin' AWOL."

"George that sounds like the only way we can settle this, but it sure don't make me happy."

"I've got a few things stashed in the stable that I'll give you and you can sell, but you should probably get Aunte to do it 'cause I don't want you goin' across the river I'd think they'd bring close to a hundred dollars."

"Whatever we gotta do to keep you from getting' hung is what we'll do."

While the whole world seemed to be falling in around George, some things went right. He knew he needed a better horse and outfit than the cavalry had and on top of that he didn't want to do more than go AWOL. Stealing a horse just wouldn't set well with the Army. The last day of the month fell on Friday and it gave him a two day jump on his mission.

Friday's also meant that San Angelo would be packed and there would be a lot of horses on the street and the owners would be deeply involved in the vice that was offered there.

At about ten o'clock, George got out of bed and kissed Ellen good-bye. He slipped into the common clothes that Ellen had stolen from the laundry. George had hugged and kissed the children as a departing father would, before he put them to bed, but he had to go back into their room and observe them for a last time before he left for what he knew would be a long time.

He strapped on the .45 Colt and holster he had taken from a cattle rustler and conveniently forgotten to turn in and picked up the Henry that he had liberated the same way. George slung the saddle bag, that Ellen had so carefully packed with items for the trip, over his shoulder. He turned and made his way toward the door in the dark.

When he reached the door he was surprised to see Ellen standing there. She held out her arms and said, "Give me a last kiss. I hate to see you go, but I know it's for the best. You've left many a time and I knew it could be for the last time, but for some reason this here seems to be harder."

She melted into his arms and started to cry.

"You can't be doin' that. I is havin' enough trouble as it is. You put all your worrin' into Georgia and Crawford. Bring us another good one and love it for me as well as you. I ain't gone forever. I promise I'll send you some money somehow and I'll see you when I can at your pa's."

He briefly kissed her and held her tight. He knew he could not linger long as he had Walt and Nero to meet by the gate at 11 o'clock.

They were at the gate and the three of them walked past the guard who snapped a brisk salute and then extended their hands and wished the three God speed. They crossed the Concho and carefully made their way into the darkened streets. The three walked mostly in the shadows of the buildings and avoided getting close to windows where the light was coming from.

George found young and stout looking gilding, untied him and led him rapidly to the outskirts of town. He was soon met by Walt and Nero both of them had selected their mounts and they headed east to where they knew there was a crossing back to the north side of the Concho.

The men had ridden this territory probably as much are more than anyone and put their knowledge to good use. The headed north as rapidly as possible and continued until they reached a spring that they had previously mapped for the government. Just as they had planned, it was just past sunup when they arrived at their destination.

In the daylight they reappraised their horses and found that all the years in the saddle had at least taught them how to judge an animal, even in the dark. The problem with the horses were that they all carried brands. This was feared to be a problem in the future, but they hoped to solve that by getting new mounts as soon as possible.

"Sergeant, looks like at least the first part of our plan has worked like it had axle grease. I sure hope the other boy's plans work as well."

"Listen to me good boys. You will never again call me Sergeant. I am George and that is that and you two are Walter and Nero. We can never again step back into our past. Now let's let the horses rest and graze and all get a little sleep. This evening we should head for Kansas and then hope we disappear like the shadows in the night."

As they sat around the small campfire and finished their coffee and bacon, George said, "You know instead of headin' north I think we should just hole up here for a few days. The thing we need most is money and this spring is goin' to have travelers stoppin'. We know that most of the travelers in this area are horse thieves or bandits trying to get back to Mexico or San Angelo. So, let's just set here for a day or two and see what is brought to us. Maybe we can pick up come money from some of these thievin' bastards.

"There is a small meadow on the other side of the ridge. Take the horses there and hobble 'em. We don't want to give away our surprise."

They placed there bed rolls in the trees and took turns getting sleep. There waiting game had begun and the time passed slowly, but the rest the men were able to secure made them feel better and more confident that they had made the right decision.

The men took turns scanning the valley with the spyglass that George had not returned from their last scouting trip, but nothing appeared.

About mid-day on their second day in the trees, Nero suddenly motioned to the others. "There's a wagon train a commin'"

The men scurried into position and hoped that the train would bring them what they needed.

The men were positioned out of sight, but were able to hear some of the conversation coming from the people in the four wagons as they watered their horse and filled their water barrels.

It was obvious that these were sodbusters coming from Kansas and were looking for a new site to settle.

When the group started discussing staying the night by the spring, George stood up and approached the wagons.

"Folks, you has got your water, but you need to be movin' on. I'm a Texas Ranger and there is some real bad murdin', thieves in this area and me and my boys is layin' up here for 'em. So if you'd move on down the trail a piece it'd be real helpful."

The startled look on the faces, were soon followed by a scurry of activity. They quickly gathered the things that they had removed and hurled them into the wagons.

Not a word was spoken until the lead wagon driver slapped the reins on his horses and turned toward George and said, "Good luck to yah."

As they left George said to the others, "We ain't robbin' no one that we has been protectin' all these years. Time will bring us what we is a needin."

The men resumed their position and continued their wait.

Their patience paid off the next morning when George picked up dust in the far distance. He held his focus on the approaching riders until he could make out their faces.

"Boys you ain't gonna believe this, those bastard Kirbys that we has been chasin' for all this time is a ridin' right to us. We'd better get are shootin' hands ready, cause you know they ain't gonna go down easy. You two get in the rocks and stay down, have 'em carbines ready and I'll do the talkin'."

George took a seat near the biggest tree in the area with his Henry cradled in his arms. The shadow of the tree helped him blend in perfectly with the surroundings.

The Kirbys rode in at a fast gallop. They knew the spring and were more than anxious to quench their thirst. They dismounted and rushed to the

cool refreshing pool and fell on their stomachs and pushed their faces into the welcome refreshment.

George stood and when he felt the time was right levered a cartridge into the chamber. The sound of the action did exactly what he had hoped it would and the men all froze in their prone position.

"Now boys if you will just be so kind as to keep a layin' where you is, it would be deeply appreciated. If you don't do that, you will probably keep that position 'till the Devil comes and gets you."

The prone men slowly strained their necks upward to try to see who had so easily got the drop on them. One of the men rose up on his hands and that was all it took for George to send a round into the spring that send a spray of water over the men.

"I said, stay down!"

The man immediately fell flat on the ground.

"Now some of my men is gonna come round and take your irons. The rest of 'em is gonna keep the front sights on the top of your heads so don't give 'em any cause to pull the trigger."

While Nero and Walter were removing the pistols, George walked over to the horses and started going through the saddlebags. He found several leather pokes and one large canvas bag that was nice and hefty.

"Now gentlemen if you will stand we will be takin' your holsters and be goin' through your pockets. We sure don't want to be missin' nothin'. When that's done you'll please remove your boots and give 'em to my boys."

Finally, one of the men said, "What in the hell do you niggers think you is a doin'?"

"Here's the way I see it, you Kirby bastards has robbed and murdered so many folks that we is doin' you a favor. We is leavin' you here at the water hole and fixin' it so you don't want to leave. If I know the patrols one of 'em will be along in a day or two and will be glad to take you back to Fort Concho. I think they'll have a surprise for you when you get there.

"Now, if you try to walk out of here I promise you want get far. Those rocks are mighty sharp and once you have all you can stand you'll be too far from water. So set tight and just wait for the Cavalry to get here. They been lookin' for you for a long time and I'm sure they'll be happy to see you."

"You black sons-of-bitches; if we ever get a chance we'll kill you. You have messed with the wrong bunch."

"I ain't fearin' that none too much. The charges against you should keep you occupied for more years than I expect to be alive."

They kicked their horses and left the barefoot bunch standing by the pool. As they rode away several rocks were sent their way, but no harm done.

The boys went to the meadow on the other side of the ridge and picked up their horses, then headed at full gallop on to the north. They rode for about an hour and came to a grove of trees on a dry creek bank.

They spread a blanket on the ground and emptied all of the pokes and the canvas bag on it and started to count what they had. It came to twelve hundred and twenty-two dollars and forty-two cents.

"Damn, those boys has been busy and must have made some pretty good hits." George stopped for a minute and then said, "We sure do thank 'em for

all of their good work."The men broke out in laughter not only for their good fortune, but because they for the first time in several months felt that things were going their way.

"Let's go through the horses and see if we can come up with some better mounts and some that ain't branded. When we get through lets rest for a while and then hit the trail. With the food those Kirby's were carryin' we can last several days. When we get to Kansas I think we should split up. The three of us together are too easy spotted."

After the three departed George headed toward east Kansas he stopped several places and took small jobs. The non-killing skills he had learned in the Army served him well. He was a good carpenter and mason and with all the construction, driven by new settlers, he was able to make day money that covered his expenses.

When he thought that enough time had passed he went to the Post Of-fice in Wichita and sent three hundred dollars by post to Luge. He had the clerk in his hotel write this letter which he enclosed in the package.

"Dear Ellen,

I am sending you enough money to keep you and the kids for a good time. I will come by the farm soon.

My love to all.

George"

The End